For Angie —   *Sept 2019*

Borderline Hero
A Novel

It's a neverending story —
unfortunately

KENNETH KONECNIK

Best wishes,   *Ken*

authorHOUSE®

AuthorHouse™
1663 Liberty Drive
Bloomington, IN 47403
www.authorhouse.com
Phone: 1-800-839-8640

Published by AuthorHouse 01/24/2014

ISBN: 978-1-4918-5578-2 (sc)
ISBN: 978-1-4918-5577-5 (hc)
ISBN: 978-1-4918-5576-8 (e)

Library of Congress Control Number: 2014901137

*May young people with fiery passions to change
the world never succumb to indifference.*

CHAPTER 1

THE CELEBRATION BEGAN AT SUNRISE. The town of Sugarfield, Texas was closed for business, school bells were silenced and traffic was re-routed. Instead of car tunes and assorted phone rings, firecrackers sizzled and cracked. Balloons bobbed and weaved. Batons twirled and trumpets blared as marching bands stepped off, luring the beaming crowds from the town square to the Ft. Bend County Fairgrounds for a day of patriotic festivities.

To the surprise of one uneasy observer, the view of the fairgrounds went from pleasant to fascinating to stupendously queasy as the rising Ferris Wheel car came to an abrupt, swaying stop at the top of the giant ride. Curtis Moultrie, making the most of a day without algebra class, grabbed hold of his "steady," Jillian, as she nearly came flying out of her seat. "Easy, my dear. We are alone at last!" intoned an enraptured Curtis, in easily his finest melodramatic performance of the day.

"Relax, big boy," Jillian replied. "One slip, and you'll end up down in the cotton candy booth."

"All the better to present you with the sweetness you deserve, my beauty! Where may I take you next?"

"Ground floor. Now!" answered a sufficiently amused Jillian.

"Alright. Please keep your hands and arms inside the ride," instructed Curtis," and off your fellow passengers!"

"Yeah, right," deadpanned Jillian.

"Next stop," Curtis called out...."planet earth!"

They spent the rest of the afternoon hand in hand, exploring the grounds as Curtis rang the bell as a strongman, won Jillian a kewpie doll for sharp-shooting and chased her around the Merry-Go-Round on his mighty stag, then joined the rest of his family in final celebration of the day that changed the course of history for each and every one of the happy revelers, forever.

The night sky lit up like a Christmas tree. Brilliant red, green and blue starbursts erupted from out of the blackness, then in slow motion turned into glittering, twinkling teardrops fluttering and falling to the horizon as mini rat-a-tat explosions gave way to one final "ka-boom!" All heads followed the descent in unison, eyes and mouths equally in awe, the "oooos" and "ahhhhs" intermingling.

"Isn't it wonderful," asked Jenny Moultrie of no one in particular, leaning back in her lawn chair, ready for the next salvo.

"The best, Jenny dear," reassured her husband, Jeb, proudly eyeing their three children whose excitement was written all over their faces, with the exception of son, Curtis. "Curt, partner, you don't seem to be enjoying Independence Day."

Curtis Moultrie appeared as though his mind was on his 1973 Mustang or his constant companion, Jillian. He was thinking of neither. "Somehow it doesn't seem right dad," explained Curtis.

"Not right, son? What's not right about celebrating our independence?"

"I mean it just doesn't seem right celebrating our independence on the 11th of May.

"Curtis," as Jeb Moultrie patiently explained, "we've been celebrating this day this way for three years now - since you were a freshman. You know that."

"I know," replied a reluctant Curtis. "I guess I just associate fireworks displays and patriotic celebrations with the Fourth of July. It was different then."

"Curtis, my man, you know those days are over. Texas is a sovereign nation once again!"

"What's the Fourth of July?" little Camilla wanted to know.

"Camilla, honey, that was from a different time," explained dad. "You were only three. We were part of a bigger country then."

"How come we aren't now?" questioned Camilla.

It was Jeb Junior (JJ for short) who clarified recent history. "Because we wanted to be on our own, Squeaky. We got tired of big government running our lives, ignoring our values and making us do things we didn't want to do."

"But *you* tell me what to do, JJ."

"That's different, Squeaky, that's totally different!"

As the grand finale tore apart the nighttime sky, Jenny Moultrie jumped up in excitement. "I'm as happy as a lark. Let's celebrate! Let's visit the new neighbors tomorrow!"

Curtis was in favor, but apprehensive. "Aren't they from up north? Is that a good idea?"

Jeb Moultrie considered the question, then replied: "Let's find out."

CHAPTER 2

Speaking before the House of Representatives in Austin, President Jefferson McCall of the new Republic of Texas issued a declaration of freedom.

"My fellow conservative Texans, three years ago this May, we took our country back from oppressive rule, immoral legislation and taxation without representation. We gave our great land back to the people to be governed by themselves, for themselves, unto themselves according to our new Constitution and to the Almighty. This historic action has echoed throughout the countryside, cities and communities of this place we call home, which now totals over 26,000,000 God-fearing, hard-charging, straight-shooting Texans!"

The applause was spontaneous, ear-splitting and universal.

"Our peaceful and righteous return to sovereignty has transferred the reins of governance from the elitists and big-government bureaucrats in Washington to the duly elected representatives of the people here assembled. The negotiated terms of our separation allowed for the exchange of goods, services and travel between the Republic of Texas and the United States of America, each country maintaining its own verified borders, laws, currency and standing armies.

The Republic of Texas proudly draws its strength from our people, our culture and from the total and unconditional support of individual liberty, family values and Christian fellowship. As God is our witness, we shall forever defend the right – and the responsibility – to bear arms, bear children and bear the image of no other God before us.

We are a nation of <u>legal citizens </u>who are proud of our land; who are proud to work for a living; who believe in swift justice for aliens; and who firmly believe that abortion is a sin and that marriage is defined as the union of one man and one woman, according to the Scriptures."

The joyous, celebratory response reached to the highest rafters.

"We support our militia at all our borders and in any future action which may be deemed necessary to protect the ideals, rights and freedoms of our just cause. Our Declaration of Freedom is undeniable and unwavering."

From high above, the Gadsden flag with coiled serpent and slogan was unfurled. Designed by Gen. Christopher Gadsden in 1775, it has long been a symbol of support for civil liberties. As the brilliant yellow flag slowly descended, President McCall shouted out its emblazoned motto: *"Don't Tread on Me!"*

The House of Representatives exuberantly rose as one, filling the room with cheers of unbridled fervor, the duration of which had not been experienced since an outdoor celebration of another historic political event took place on the evening of November 12, 2008 in the city of Chicago.

CHAPTER 3

AT 6-FOOT SEVEN AND 287 pounds, Frank Kazmarczyk was one of the best collegiate defensive ends in the state. His sheer strength, quick feet and football instincts were surpassed only by his aptitude for aeronautical engineering, which made him eligible for two of America's greatest industries: aerospace and the NFL. Looking at the big picture through realistic glasses, Frank decided he'd be better off in the long run building rockets rather than trying to bulldoze his way through 300-pound linemen on the way to the quarterback. His college sweetheart, and new bride Emma, concurred. Although some say it was the other way around.

Of all the offers Frank received, the best one by far combined a great starting salary with immediate propulsion design opportunities and a warmer climate. One week after their honeymoon, Frank and Emma packed their bags and memories of Ames, Iowa and headed south. Two days later they arrived at the outskirts of their new home as they crossed the United States border into Texas.

Their house was bright and cheery and they were in their second day of unpacking clothes and organizing the kitchen when the doorbell rang. After stepping over boxes and clearing a pathway, Frank opened the front door to the delight of a family of five standing outside, grins and gifts in hand.

"Howdy neighbor," exclaimed the exuberant Texan. "I'm Jeb Moultrie. This here's my wife Jenny, sons JJ, Curtis and little Camilla."

Frank was a bit overwhelmed, but managed a simple "Hello, I'm Frank Kazmarczyk."

"Oh my... Hello," replied Jenny, simultaneously processing Frank's size and lineage with some difficulty.

Frank pressed on. "And this is Emma. We're married. I mean we just got married. I mean we're newlyweds!"

"Of course you are, Frank and Emma," insisted Jeb. "Welcome to the neighborhood!"

Camilla jumped to the front of the line. "We brought you a pecan pie! It's our favorite!"

Emma knelt down to take the proudly offered gift. Well thank you, Camilla. I'm sure we'll like it too!"

Frank invited the Moultries into the living room, which still was strewn with unopened moving boxes, as Emma verified the obvious, "We're not settled in yet." JJ was immediately drawn to one giant cardboard box overflowing with bronze-plated figures and footballs. "Shoot," he blurted out, "look at all them trophies! What position did you play, Frank?"

"Defensive end," answered Frank.

"You must've had a lot of sacks," acknowledged JJ as he examined the temporary trophy case.

"A few," offered Frank.

Emma quickly clarified Frank's reluctant reply while giving him a motivating tap on his backside. "Frank led the league in high school and college!"

"Why didn't you turn pro big guy?" asked an impressed JJ.

"I tore up my knee a little in my senior year, JJ. Plus, I like the game, but I didn't want it to define my life. I had bigger plans."

"And what did those plans turn out to be, if you don't mind my asking?" inquired Jeb.

"My degree is in aeronautical engineering," answered Frank.

"Geez," Jeb reacted, you're a rocket scientist! Jenny, we got a rocket scientist for a neighbor!"

Camilla's eyes got as big as the plate she brought the pecan pie on. "Are you going to the moon, Mr.Kazmarczyk?" Will you take me?"

"I'm not an astronaut, Camilla," explained Frank with an engaging smile. "I'm just going to help build their rocket ships. Besides, I think our next stop is Mars!"

Camilla loved it all the more. "Mars! Wow!"

Jenny had a question of her own. "And how about you, Emma? What are your *big plans* for the future?"

"I'm an elementary school science teacher. I want to help the next generation catch up with China and Russia and other countries. There's no reason we shouldn't be the leader in scientific knowledge," elucidated Emma.

"I see," Jenny softly replied, resisting the urge to comment on the over-emphasis of scientific thought in Texas classrooms.

Jeb abruptly got around to the big question. "So, what made you two decide to do all that good work here in the Republic of Texas? Was it our wide open spaces, our 40-ounce steaks or our good Christian upbringing?"

Frank nodded, "All of those things had something to do with it, Jeb. But mainly I saw opportunity here. The United States may have pulled NASA out of Texas, but the folks down here still know something about aerospace. The companies that remained had some good openings – so we're here!"

"To hell with NASA," snapped Jeb. "Houston doesn't have a problem without NASA, NASA has a problem without Houston, believe you me!" Who needs 'em! Did you know that the Texas economy is so huge we are the equivalent of the *eleventh largest country* in the world. Did you know that, Frank? Did you?"

"Plus, chimed in JJ, we got the best football anywhere! You should see our Sugarfield boys take the field, Frank!"

"I'd like to," replied Frank.

JJ followed right up with, "How about Friday, big guy?"

"Friday?" repeated Frank, surprised by the urgency.

"Friday Night Lights, Frank. High school football at its best! Where do you think the expression *Friday Night Lights* came from? Join us. We got a group of good ol' boys who come out every week to watch the game. They'd love to meet a big-time jock like you."

"Did they play football, too?" asked Frank.

"Some of them," answered JJ. "But all of them are part of something even bigger around here. You might want to think about joining it yourself."

"And what would that be, JJ?"

JJ paused for effect, then watched for Frank's reaction as he answered, "McCall's Militia!"

The tailgating started across the street from the Sugarfield High football field in Carl Wiggins' back yard. Alcoholic beverages were not allowed around school property, but Carl was not similarly constrained. Carl's doors were open to anyone who supported Sugarfield High Football, the new Republic of Texas and the Militia from which it sprang. Everyone brought their own refreshment of choice and sat in lawn chairs around a mile-high pile of taco chips, a punch bowl full of salsa and a grill loaded with burgers and brats.

The group consisted of a dozen football-crazed fanatics from a wide range of ages and backgrounds. Carl, an electrician, had graduated from Sugarfield ten years earlier. Other alums included Ben, who was a carpenter. "Slippery" Pete was a plumber. The Wilson twins ran a hardware store. There also was a veterinarian, a postman, a waste management collector and several military veterans, including Zeke Hogan, an infantry sergeant from the Iraq war.

Frank Kazmarczyk was greeted with open arms. "Any friend of JJ's is a friend of ours," declared Ben.

"Even if you are a Yankee," nudged "Slippery" Pete.

"Well, I'm here now. Thanks!" Frank responded. "And glad to be here, too. It's a great place to live. Great people, too. Emma and I couldn't be happier."

"We heard you played some football. We're a little partial to the game ourselves," "Slippery" continued.

"So I see," answered Frank. "Yep, I played defensive end."

"We could use you in Cowboys Stadium right now!"

"I'm afraid I'm not what I used to be, guys."

"Hey, who is?" ol' Carl agreed. "But you know, one place we really could use your services is right here in our band of brothers: "McCall's Militia.""

Frank paused for a moment, then asked, "What does that involve, Carl?"

"Not a whole lot. Every county has its own regiment, so there are a lot of other men involved. We meet every Sunday evening for a couple of hours. Then every other month we spend a weekend on the road doing border checks. The Texas Rangers are on duty full-time and the National Guard goes out on regularly scheduled patrols. We're kind of like a backup. We keep our eyes and ears open. In an emergency, if the President calls, we go."

Frank considered the pros and cons. On the one hand, he felt some obligation to the place where he was earning a good living, and he wanted his neighbors to feel that he was committed to the cause. On the other hand, he would be giving up some free time, but not that much in the grand scheme of things. A little taste of military life might be an interesting experience, he thought. So he did what military men over the years have always advised *against* doing: he volunteered.

With militia business out of the way, the conversation returned to the merits of the two opposing quarterbacks, the running backs and most important of all, the defense!

"Defense wins championships, Frank, you know that!" argued Zeke.

"I like to think so," Frank fired back.

"You've got to shut down the *enemy* and I mean shut him down good! Make him think twice about entering your territory. Take him down and take him out! Period! That's how we did it in Iraq!"

"Okay, Zeke, how about another burger for the road, buddy," interjected their host, trying to tamp down the veteran's mounting rage. "It's time for kickoff!"

Everybody scurried around picking up plates and chairs and shutting down the grill, then headed across the street for some action. Although from Frank's perspective, at least one person appeared to have already seen more than enough.

CHAPTER 4

CURTIS MOULTRIE AND JILLIAN CLINE knew each other since the fifth grade. In those days, Curtis didn't see much point in making friends with someone who couldn't swing a baseball bat, catch spiders or shoot BB guns very well, although if he had given her half a chance, he would have found out otherwise.

It was only later, when they got to high school that Curtis got to know the real Jillian. One day between classes, Jillian suddenly appeared at Curtis's locker and popped the question: "Hey Curtis, a group of us are going on a hayride this Friday night and we thought – I thought – you might want to go with me – with us. We'll toast some marshmallows, too!"

Before Curtis could think of saying, "I've got a game, I've got homework, or a hayride sounds boring," he said what any guy would say who wasn't prepared for a surprise attack like this as he blurted out, "Okay, fine."

It was the first of many memorable dates between two people who hit it off in every way, as Curtis discovered he had met his match in flag football, clever online postings and "Angry Hamsters." Jillian was a cute, perky, bright-eyed brunette laugh track. She made Curtis feel like he was the coolest, wittiest guy on the face of the earth. When he was with Jillian, Curtis felt smart, confident and totally in control. He never knew what hit him.

To Jillian, the only thing more appealing than Curtis's outgoing personality and dimple-cheeked good looks was his inquisitive mind and sense of purpose. He liked going to class. His favorite subjects were history and social studies. Math and science were okay, but Curtis was more interested in the human element rather than the Table of Elements, the chemistry that existed between himself and Jillian, notwithstanding.

Most of their dates were impromptu and started out in the usual way, with Curtis asking the usual question: "So, what do you want to do tonight, kiddo?"

Jillian was always prepared: "I was thinking a movie."

Curtis knew her type. "Vampires don't show up till after 8 o'clock, Jillian. Until then I would be more than happy to suck…your…blood!" as he dived toward her neck.

"Curtis!" feigned a horrified Jillian. "Let's do dinner first."

"Okay," obliged Curtis. "Where?"

"How about Italian?" asked Jillian.

"*Bellissima*!" reacted a debonair Curtis, putting his scrunched up fingers to his lips and blowing them away with a kiss.

Jillian asked for clarification. "Does that mean, *good?*"

"It sounds good, doesn't it? *Bellissima!*" It rolls right off my tongue, *Bel-liss-ima!*"

"So does the spaghetti the way you eat it. You're not supposed to cut it with your fork, you twirl it in your spoon, Signor Curtis!"

"Okay, now you got me thinking, "Mexican!" countered Curtis.

"What happened to *Bellissima?*" chided Jillian.

"Nah, I'm kind of liking *Bueno*. Sounds good, doesn't it, *Bueno!*… the way it jumps right out of my mouth…*Bueno, Senorita! Bueno!*

They agreed to enchiladas. Saw vampires. Then kissed, lingered and softly murmured, "Good night."

CHAPTER 5

JENNY MOULTRIE WAS A SOUTHERN Baptist belle who instilled in her family the manners and values that she and most everyone else in Ft. Bend County believed in with a passion. A firm believer in the Bible, the sanctity of life and the institution of marriage, Jenny proudly held court at numerous coffees in her home and in meetings at Sugarfield Middle School, where she was President of the Parent-Teachers Association.

It was in this capacity that Jenny kept an eagle eye on the science of evolution being taught in school, a concept decidedly at odds with the basic principles of the new Republic. "Man did not evolve from some form of sea life that crawled up onto the earth. And we are absolutely, positively *not* descendants of apes! How disgusting!" an exasperated Jenny was often heard to exclaim. To prove her point, she would read passages from her Bible: "*In the beginning, God created the heavens and the earth. The Lord God formed a man from the dust of the ground and breathed into his nostrils the breath of life. Then the Lord God made a woman from the rib he had taken out of the man. Genesis: 1-2.*"

Jenny would conclude with a flourish: "There was no Big Bang explosion billions of years ago that led to life on earth. That is merely a theory being put forward by people who are trying to explain the universe without a Creator. The facts, as we Christians know them, are that life began with Adam and Eve less than 5,000 years ago. The earth was fully formed and beautiful, teeming with all manner of plants and animals. But there *was* sin. And there *was* a Great Flood. Noah built an arc and saved the animal kingdom and mankind from itself, not from some giant meteor from outer space. There *was* no catastrophic impact! There *is* no global warming! These are the lessons that our young people should be learning! There is a place for science in the classroom, but not at the expense of our sacred Christian beliefs."

Sitting in the back of the room, new neighbor Emma began considering the impact of today's lesson: teaching modern science would be a tricky business in the Republic of Texas.

Jenny's biggest supporter was her husband, Jeb. He shared her family values across the board. It was what brought them together in the first place, twenty-five years earlier. Back then, Jeb was the owner of a small construction company that built and remodeled offices, which happened to include the daycare center that Jenny helped run.

The basic plans for re-modeling the reception area and play rooms were drawn up by Jenny, and brought to life by Jeb Moultrie Construction. It was only a six-month project, but in that time, amid the dust and confusion, Jeb was taken by Jenny's natural connection with children, as she helped them play games, paint pictures, sing songs and respect the golden rule, as all good Christians do.

Nearly every day, after all the carpenters, electricians and painters young and old had gone home, Jeb and Jenny would go out - sometimes to the movies, sometimes to dinner, sometimes for long walks or rides in the park. Whatever they talked about came natural to them both: the importance of family and following the rules; being responsible and accountable for one's life; following through on the hopes and dreams for the future in a land where they could work, prosper and enjoy life, according to God's plan. They went from agreeing with, to liking a lot, to loving each other madly, as it had seemed destined to be.

God's plan, as is turned out, included a small home in Sugarfield, which Jeb immediately enlarged to include a family room and sun deck; a major step forward into designing and building condominiums by Jeb Moultrie Construction; and three children, each as different from the other as they could possibly be.

How such different and distinct personalities could emerge from the same household was anybody's guess. There was no rhyme or reason for the fact that Jenny and Jeb's middle son, Curtis, was as independent, as curious and as questioning as he was. Curtis didn't take anything at face value. He had to feel it in his bones. He didn't purposely play devil's advocate, he just wanted to hear all sides and come to his own conclusion. This made Curtis a very good student in high school social studies, civics and of life. He was the only Moultrie to question the validity of the new Republic.

Camilla was only in first grade. She was great at spelling, addition and subtraction, and had a lot of fun at recess. Camilla was the apple of her mother's eye and was following in her footsteps by instantly joining any conversation and speaking her mind. She would never outgrow her nickname, "Squeaky."

Number-one son, Jeb Jr. was a chip off the old block, and then some. JJ was a firm believer in the Moultrie family values of hard work and proper living. After high school, JJ bought himself a Ford 350 Dually 4X4 truck with a big 6.4 liter V-8 engine to cart around all the equipment he bought for his new landscaping business. JJ worked from dawn to dusk planting flowers and trees, trimming shrubs and power washing house eaves, windows and sidewalks. He did good work and met lots of new people in the process. He became friends with many other service-oriented workers in the area who rooted for the same teams, hunted for the same game and supported the same causes that were the basis of the new Republic: freedom from big government and its overreaching health care laws; gun control; same-sex marriage; and the problems closest to JJ's heart… ungodly abortion laws, clinics and lax immigration control.

JJ had been known to get a little carried away in these matters, and one day he flew off the handle as though he had been struck by lightning. What started out like just another fun phone call from his girlfriend Rita, turned into a scenario that JJ simply could not abide by. Rita was pregnant, and she wanted an abortion, which everyone knew was morally wrong and totally illegal in the Republic of Texas.

CHAPTER 6

OUTLAWING ABORTION IN THE NEW Republic was handled with one stroke of President McCall's pen. Eliminating illegal immigration took considerably more effort. The Texas border with Mexico is over 1,200 miles long and has 18 Ports of Entry along the way. Nearly all of these checkpoints are connected to major highways, so as soon as individuals gain entry, the impact of their presence is felt everywhere across the new Republic of Texas.

When this border was controlled by the United States of America, crossing it was not difficult. Entry papers were easy to come by. Security was lax in the more remote areas. Just about anyone who wanted to enter the states, entered the states. Thousands came secretly by train, riding in and on boxcars and hiding in the automobiles being transported by rail from factories in Mexico to the US market. Across desolate plains, Mexican drug cartel dealers, El Salvador gangs, and other Central American foreigners found easy entry to a land of easy pickin's for their particular brand of drugs, crime and violence.

In those days, illegal immigration was often debated but never effectively resolved. The only people who really seemed to care were those who personally had to deal with the problem. The violence near the border crossings had Texas families terrified and feeling helpless. The rampant drug trafficking had communities living in fear for their loved ones. The influx of illegal immigrant workers put many Texans out of a job. The "political correctness" of the rest of the country allowed millions of minorities to enter, live in and enjoy the benefits of the United States without being legal citizens of the United States. These issues resonated with the other southern states, and to a degree, with some of the plains states as well as rural areas in the north. This is why there was no universal outcry across the country when Texas regained its independence. On the contrary, many residents and organized religious groups in like-minded, conservative states actually picked up and moved to the new Republic, where in many ways, they felt more at home.

The ultimate solution to the immigration problem had to come from the people who were mostly directly affected. And finally it did. One of the Republic's first new laws was the Illegal Aliens Act, which called for the conscription and deportation of all illegal immigrants throughout the Republic of Texas.

Implementing the law became the responsibility of McCall's Militia, which was nationalized by President Jefferson McCall. Chief among this newly created band of eager, well-trained militia men was the Ft. Bend County Regiment under the command of Captain Jeb Moultrie of Sugarfield.

CHAPTER 7

THE MOULTRIE FAMILY HAD BEEN attending the Redeemer Baptist Church since Jeb and Jenny were married there 25 years ago. Actually, Jenny had been a member even longer, as she used to attend with her parents, Billy and Betty Jo Taylor, who were near retirement and lived just a few blocks away. Jeb's mom and dad had been killed in a car accident near the Mexican border 20 years earlier, so he felt especially close to the Taylors. Every Sunday all seven members of the immediate Moultrie family would fill half of the second pew on the right in "Moultrie Row" as every Redeemer Baptist Church goer affectionately referred to it.

The church was always filled to capacity with an attentive, devout audience. They came to visit, pray and delight in another dramatic and inspirational performance by the Rev. Thomas Meriwether. His most recent sermon, entitled "A Life to Cherish" was delivered with all the unbridled fury and passion the Reverend was famous for throughout Ft. Bend County.

"Life is the most precious gift in the entire universe," he began. "At the very moment - that millisecond - when life is created, something truly miraculous occurs. A flash of brilliance - a spark of incomprehensible power - as the outstretched arm and fingertips of God Almighty render life out of nothingness! A living, breathing entity of multitudinous cells, tissues and complex organs surround a soul of unexplored depth and beauty. It is a life unlike any other, a being unto itself. A life both sacred and fallible…it is a glimpse into eternity! This profound creation must be cherished, loved and protected from inception to the end of time. Let no man judge its essence. Let no man take what was never his. Let no man play the Creator!"

The feeling of jubilation and electricity among the congregation was palpable, as heads nodded, jaws set and tears flowed. The silent benediction that followed was anything but silent in the hearts and minds of those present. These feelings carried over into dinner at the Moultries, where the joy of the morning's proceedings was embellished by the fine table proudly set by Jenny and her mother, featuring roast turkey with collard greens, black-eyed peas, grits, biscuits and gravy, pitchers of sweet tea and a choice of key lime or sweet potato pie.

The dinner conversation traditionally evolved around the State of the Republic, the state of the family, and to the chagrin of Curtis and JJ, the state their girlfriends. The unanimous view was that the transition back to Texas independence was inevitable. Big government had shown its inability to understand and consider local Texans' beliefs, feelings and traditions.

From the perspective of Gramps Taylor, the Lone Star State was always a land of basic beliefs and God-given freedoms. As Billy Taylor often volunteered. "You can't round us up, fence us in and break us down. The chances of changing us are slim to none and slim just rode out of town."

Everyone in the Republic of Texas felt more than capable of taking care of themselves. "You did a nice job remodeling the kitchen, Jeb" Betty Jo observed.

"Well, thank you, mother Taylor. It's what I do!" Jeb proudly replied. "Your daughter didn't marry no couch potato!"

"Except when it's kickoff time!" countered Jenny.

"Well, that's different," answered Jeb, scanning the room for understanding, and receiving a table full of nodding heads in return.

People like the Moultries never wanted a government watchdog looking over their shoulder or robbing from Peter to pay for Paul's responsibilities. The redistribution of wealth was not going to fly in the new Republic. "You going to eat that last biscuit, Curtis?" asked JJ.

"I'm working on it, JJ."

"Come on, give it up now. I'm starving down here!" pleaded JJ.

"You don't look like you're starving, sweet cheeks," chided Rita, giving him a not-so-gentle jab in his midsection.

The social programs instituted by the United States government no longer existed here. Social Security was added up closed down. All Texas retirees who had been receiving Social Security payments settled for a negotiated, one-time, lump-sum settlement from the United States. Call it a severance package from an institution they no longer wanted to be part of. People who were still working for a living had to make their own retirement plan and were advised to save their money or invest it in the stock market, as Pres. George W. Bush had once proposed.

Medicare was shut down and replaced with a voucher system. Each person over the age of 65 had been given a voucher for a certain amount of money based on their net worth to purchase the health care coverage they needed from an insurance company of their choosing. The plan had long been supported by the Republican Party and had been implemented by the new Republic.

"I'm looking forward to retirement," acknowledged Billy, as the dinner conversation wore on. "I think if I put my mind to it, I can catch every bass in Lake Somerville!" All the Moultries got a big laugh over that one.

"I'd like to go to Hawaii," Betty Jo quietly admitted, as the familial tone turned from raucous to sweet.

"Golden years, here we come!" announced Billy, wrapping his arm around Betty Jo as they both raised their glasses in a toast to the future.

Universal health care was similarly scuttled. Texans were perfectly happy choosing their own doctor and making their own healthcare decisions, thank you very much. In their view, it wasn't the role of the government to cover every uninsured citizen at the expense of the insured. It was up to each and every individual to pull themselves up by their bootstraps and get a life, get a job, get insurance.

On the subject of the economy, the Republic of Texas still maintained a vigorous aerospace industry that competed in the US market, and it continued to pump billions of gallons of Texas crude for itself and for export. Over the past three years, some corporations did shutter a few branch offices across the state, and tourism wasn't what it used to be. But the housing market was relatively stable, as the anti-secessionist Texans who moved out of the state were replaced by ultra conservative citizens from across rural America who moved in.

By agreement with the respective leagues, the professional sports teams across Texas still suited up for battle against their arch enemies, and their fanatical fan bases became more energized and combative than ever.

When the attention turned to the younger Moultries, Camilla proudly read her "Cat got your Tongue?" book aloud, JJ routinely outlined his plans for his landscaping business - but made no mention of any issues with Rita - and Curtis triumphantly offered how excited he was to be graduating from high school, and then rocked the house with his announcement that he had just accepted a scholarship to attend Kilmer College in Evanston, Illinois in the fall.

After a moment of stunned silence, Jeb asked, "Why do you want to go all the way up there, Curtis?" "Because they've got great journalism and creative writing programs. I want to be a writer," explained Curtis. "What are you going to write about?" asked his surprised mother.

Curtis surveyed the amazed expressions on the faces surrounding him as he replied, "Oh, I'll think of something."

CHAPTER 8

ONE OF THE MAIN REASONS Emma Kasmarczyk was hired to teach seventh-grade science at Sugarfield Middle School was her fluency in Spanish. Hispanic children made up nearly half of the class and many spoke very little English or none at all.

When Emma wrote "Mrs. Kazmarczyk" on the blackboard, it turned out to be the great equalizer, as everyone in the room struggled to repeat her name, everyone, in effect, started out on the same page. Ultimately, "Good morning, Mrs. Kazmarczyk" became a response that everyone gave with great enthusiasm and confidence, secure in the knowledge that outside of the classroom, their teacher would simply and affectionately be referred to as "Mrs. K."

Where Emma came from, there was more to science than simply identifying the sun, the moon and the planets. Emma wanted to impart to her students a deeper understanding of the theory of science rather than just the facts. What caused the earth to form? How do the environments differ on the other planets? Why do these environments not support life as we know it? Could there be life somewhere in the universe? What is really out there? Why are we here?

Emma's seventh graders never had to consider these types of questions before. Are they too young to be asked? Are they too young to care? Emma didn't think so. Every classroom has a visionary or two who "get it" or who want to get it. An inquisitive one. A restless one. One who has the instincts to go beyond rote learning and try to get to the bottom of things, and perhaps become the next pioneer in scientific theory, thought and invention as we all travel through space and time.

One such precocious 12-year old whose inquisitive and calculating mind set her apart from the rest of Emma's class was Maria Estrada. She intuitively grasped science and routinely got the highest grades. She was always a chapter ahead of the class in her Earth Science textbook partly because she wanted to find out what was next, and partly because she struggled with English, as did her parents, Hector and Juanita, who spoke practically none.

As the semester progressed, so did Maria's English. She studied and practiced her new language on her own, which sped up her grasp of science even more so. Before long she was capable of discussing the basic principles of the Big Bang theory of evolution with "Mrs. K" and was even able to help Emma explain the basic thought processes to the other English-challenged students in the class in their native tongue. By the end of the term, the seventh-grade science class at Sugarfield Middle School scored the highest grades in Ft. Bend County.

Emma was proud of her accomplishments, as was Maria and her increasingly bi-lingual parents, right up to the day Captain Jeb Moultrie and McCall's Militia came to take Hector and Juanita away.

According to the provisions of the Illegal Aliens Act, children of deported immigrant parents were allowed to remain in the Republic if they were born in Texas and could find a legal resident who would take them in. The few parents who were able to leave their offspring behind did so in the hope of giving them a better life and of possibly re-joining them in the future, although the odds of entering the Republic of Texas legally were stacked against them, considering the job skill requirements, English language requirements and quota requirements that were in place in order to keep the masses on the outside, looking in.

Thus, it was a bittersweet moment for Hector and Juanita Estrada as they left on the bus to Mexico knowing their Maria had the good fortune of being offered a place in the hearts and home of Frank and Emma Kazmarczyk.

CHAPTER 9

THE NEXT TIME THE MOULTRIES all sat down for Sunday dinner it was JJ's turn to drop a bombshell. As he cleared his throat and clinked his glass, JJ announced, "The last time we sat around this table, Curtis pointed out how proud he was to be taking a trip up north in the near future."

"Right, son." Jeb quietly acknowledged, "Kilmer College."

"In Evanston, Illinois," added a disappointed Jenny.

"Well, as of tomorrow, I am shutting down JJ's Landscaping and taking a leave of absence from the militia."

"You're doing what? Why?" asked his startled dad.

JJ surveyed his tight-knit family and simply said, "Rita is pregnant."

As the bowl of sweet potatoes Jeb was passing around came crashing out of his hand, Jeb sat upright and blurted out, "Damn! What are you two thinking, JJ?"

"It just happened, dad! She only told me last week, but I'm handling it."

"What do you mean *handling it*, sweetie?" asked Jenny. "You're getting married, son?"

"Rita thinks we're too young, mom."

"Too foolish is more like it," interjected Jeb.

"Now Jeb, Rita will do the right thing. What else can she do?"

JJ squared his shoulders, set his jaw and fumed, "She's getting an abortion!"

Jenny dropped her drumstick and Jeb pounded the table with his fist as they replied in unison, "Absolutely not!" "That cannot happen young man," admonished Jeb.

"It's against God's will," Jenny reminded everyone. "Life is sacred."

"I know, mom and dad, I know. I found out where she's going for the abortion and I'm going to stop her." "Hey, big brother, it's Rita's life," interjected Curtis. "So she thinks differently. How can you impose your ideas on her?"

"Curtis Moultrie!" admonished mom. "You know abortion is a sin! Life begins at conception. How many times has Pastor Meriwether made that point?"

"Mom, women have the right to be responsible for their own bodies and lives. The Supreme Court said it's a woman's right……"

"The Supreme Court has no jurisdiction in this Republic!" advised Jeb. "Their decisions on abortion, healthcare and public prayer are all in direct conflict with our values. They no longer speak for us. *We* speak for us. And you are one of us, Curtis!"

"My point is Rita is an adult," answered Curtis. "I don't see how we can do anything about it."

"Well I do and I can," JJ replied. "There are no abortion clinics in Texas, but I found out where she's headed. Her best friend told me she found someone online who directs women to abortion clinics up north. Her name is Jennifer Nelson and her website is called Abortion Hotline for Texans. The closest clinic is up in Norman, Oklahoma. Her best friend said she left yesterday, so I'm leaving tonight."

"Be careful sweetie," said mom. "Just talk to her. She'll do the right thing."

"JJ, don't do anything stupid up there," advised Curtis. "You'll be totally on your own. Don't do anything I wouldn't do."

"I'll do what I have to, Curtis," answered JJ as he rose from the table and kissed, backslapped and hugged his family good-bye.

Under a starry sky, JJ gassed up his truck, tossed in some maps, snacks and a duffel bag and headed north on Interstate 45. Five hours later he picked up Rte. 35 outside of Dallas and soon JJ arrived at the US border. Crossing over into Oklahoma involved the usual border agent scrutiny of passport, ID and purpose of visit, which JJ acknowledged was for business reasons. The agent asked the usual questions about firearms possession, to which JJ responded in the negative, knowing full well that any perfunctory search of his vehicle would never uncover the fake floorboard where he kept his 450 Magnum and AK-47 semi-automatic rifle with 600-round clips all tucked snugly in place.

A smile crossed JJ's face as he considered the irony of entering a country that was slowly but surely eroding its citizens' second amendment right to bear arms, which was meant to protect them from a militaristic takeover of their lives such as what was occurring at this very moment, as he sardonically responded to the border agent's wave to proceed with a "Thank you, officer. Have a nice day yourself."

JJ crossed the Red River into Oklahoma around 3 AM and estimated reaching Norman at sunrise, which would give him plenty of time to find Rita at the clinic and talk some sense into her before it was too late. He would remind her of the sacredness of life, that abortion is murder, and that he loved her and would gladly marry her. There was no way he could allow Rita to abort their child in a godforsaken place like this. Regardless of the consequences, JJ was prepared to act.

The Bessler Abortion Clinic near Norman, Oklahoma was run by Dr. Jeremy Bessler and his wife, Sue. They took over the practice from the previous doctor who had opened one of the first legal abortion clinics following the 1973 Roe v. Wade decision by the Supreme Court that made abortion legal under certain circumstances.

In those days, even though the abortion issue had been settled, it was still a dangerous time for some of the early practitioners. As late as 2009 Dr. George Tiller of Wichita, Kansas, who ran one of the first national abortion clinics, was shot and killed in his church by an anti-abortion protester. This was after he had survived a bombing of his clinic in 1985 and had been shot in both arms in 1993 by another right to-life-activist.

Dr. Bessler had always wanted to make a difference for people in need, and he decided that this was the way to go in spite of the risks that still existed. His office was clean and comfortable, and on this bright and sunny day, it had three young women sitting in the waiting room reading over the abortion consent forms and state-mandated information, including a depiction of the ultra-sound viewing of the fetus that every prospective mother had to watch, under penalty of law.

Rita McMillan had struck up a conversation with one of the other women, a studious- looking dark-haired girl examining a clinic pamphlet. Suddenly, the door opened with a rush and a tall intense-looking young man stormed in and dropped his duffel bag with a resounding thud.

"JJ!" Rita exhaled. "How did you find me?"

"Your online friend, Jennifer Nelson made it real easy," answered JJ.

"This is Jennifer," said Rita, pointing to the girl she was speaking with.

"Really? And who gave you the right to interfere in our lives?"

"Rita did," responded Jennifer.

"Rita, we have to talk," JJ said forcefully.

"You want to talk now?" questioned Rita. "Isn't it a little late for that?"

As the two other women in the room huddled together, the receptionist picked up the telephone. JJ walked up to Rita and forcefully said, "Let's go!" The receptionist suddenly stood up behind her desk and said, "I called the police. They are on their way."

Rita looked at the receptionist, then at JJ, saw the look in his eyes and summoned up the words: "Alright. Fine. Let's go!"

Having just heard the words he came 500 miles to hear, JJ rushed Rita out the door and into his truck. As she sat stiffly in her seat staring straight ahead, JJ started the engine, popped the clutch and sped away from the Bessler Clinic and all its inhumane booklets and evil practices, just as an Oklahoma State Police car rounded the corner and the clinic windows blew out, the doors blew off and flames shot 50 feet into the pale blue, suddenly red and orange-colored sky.

CHAPTER 10

CURTIS MOULTRIE WASN'T A JOCK. He was okay at sports, but the popularity he gained during his four years at Sugarfield High was the result of his ability to relate to his fellow students in simpler terms: the classes and teachers they liked and didn't like; who was taking who to the prom; why the new Mustang could take the new Camaro in the quarter-mile. Day-to-day stuff. Real stuff. He was the editor of the school newspaper, so he sort of represented the student body. In fact, many of the kids who had a hard time making friends with others, became good friends with Curtis. He was a good listener and confidant. More than any other course or curriculum, Curtis Moultrie was a student of human nature. He gravitated to similar souls and noble causes, which considerably heightened the angst he immediately felt when he turned on the national television news the evening after the Moultrie family dinner and saw the breaking story of an abortion clinic bombing, followed by a description of the pickup truck, driver and passenger they were looking for.

Within seconds of Curtis calling out the news to anyone within earshot, Jenny ran into the den from the kitchen, Jeb from the garage and Camilla from her bedroom. All four became immediately transfixed by the images they were watching on TV: the bombed out building entrance; the blackened interior; the yellow-taped intersection eerily awash in flashing police car lights, gurgling fire truck engines and muffled two-way radio exchanges.

A television reporter at the scene gave a brief synopsis of the facts at hand. "At approximately 10 AM, the Bessler Abortion Clinic was firebombed by a person or persons unknown. There was one fatality and another person was critically injured. There were no eyewitnesses to the explosion, although two people of interest were seen speeding away shortly after the blast in a dark-colored pickup truck. Anyone who may have witnessed the incident is asked to contact the local authorities. Two surveillance cameras that were mounted on top of the clinic were recovered intact by the Oklahoma State Police. The FBI also has agents on the scene. Tune in for further details tonight at 6 o'clock. This is Kay Bailey, KXOTV, Norman, Oklahoma"

"Oh, Jeb! Isn't that where JJ was going?" asked a bewildered Jenny.

"I don't know. Maybe. We have to get in touch with him," Jeb replied. "Have you heard from him, Curtis?"

"I'm calling him now," answered Curtis as he hit speed dial.

After the first ring, JJ checked his Caller ID and answered. "Curtis, that you?"

"It's me," answered Curtis.

"What's going on, JJ?"

"I don't know. I just picked Rita up at the clinic and the whole place blew sky high."

"The TV news said that two people were seen fleeing the scene in a truck that sounds like yours," Curtis explained.

"Well, I guess that could be us, I didn't see what happened."

"Are you telling me you had nothing to do with this, JJ?"

"That's what I'm telling you, little brother. Put dad on the phone," ordered JJ.

Curtis handed his phone to his dad and tried to decipher what JJ was telling him. The sum total of Jeb's replies were, "Right. Okay. Good. Use Rita's phone from now on. Just in case."

"In case of what?" asked Curtis, as Jeb ended the call.

"In case someone identifies his truck and tries tracking his phone."

"Dad, what did JJ tell you?" Curtis persisted.

"Is JJ coming home? asked a flustered Camilla, sensing all was not right in their world.

"No. We're going to go get him…" answered Jeb, "…while the getting's good."

Somewhere west of Lake Thunderbird, JJ exited Interstate 35 and found his way to an old two-lane dirt road heading south. He pulled off under an ancient oak tree, shut off the engine and turned his attention to Rita for the first time since he so fitfully entered the Bessler abortion clinic in what seemed like an eternity ago.

Rita summed up her thoughts succinctly. "What in the hell are you doing, JJ?"

"Well, I thought we'd rest here a while – I've been driving all night – and figure out the best route home." "You know what I mean," insisted Rita. "That clinic disintegrated just minutes after we left. There were people in there! Someone probably died! Did you do that?"

"Rita, how could you say such a thing? I don't know what happened. I'm all shook up, too. That's not the first time something like that has happened around here. There are lunatics out there that do god-awful things. That could've been you in there when the bomb went off. Did you ever think of that? I saved you Rita."

"And now we're on the run," said Rita, pointing out the obvious.

"Well, yeah I know how this must look. But there is no proof I did anything and I'm not going to let anybody up here take me in. That would be an open-and-shut case of good ol' Texas boy bombs a clinic to keep his girlfriend from getting an abortion. Hell, they'd probably try to pin all the abortion clinic bombings on me. No sir."

"And just how do you plan on crossing the border if we get that far JJ?" asked Rita.

"I got maps. I got guns. I'll get us there, Rita."

"Really. And then what. You and what army are going to take on the United States Border Patrol? Do you want to start another civil war?"

"That wouldn't be my first choice. Let me use your phone."

After two rings, Jeb Moultrie answered his phone with a question: "JJ, you and Rita okay?"

"We're fine, dad. Are we good to go?"

"We are. Our best militia man, Zeke, and me are on the road right now. We'll cross the border around sundown at Highway 377. It's a seldom used road with only one border agent. We'll cross over, pick you up and bring you back."

As daylight grudgingly gave way to dusk, Jeb and Zeke finally approached the border crossing only to discover the one-man outpost had been reinforced with a contingent of Oklahoma State Police cruisers and a U.S. Army "deuce and a half" truck with armed soldiers thoroughly checking every vehicle that was going into the United States and every vehicle that was entering the Republic of Texas.

Jeb didn't know what he was going to tell JJ, who was sitting patiently in his truck with Rita 25 miles to the north. Until he formulated another plan, Jeb dialed Rita's number and simply said: "Stand by. We've got an issue here."

No sooner had JJ hung up when he suddenly heard the buzzing propeller of a small airplane getting louder by the second. He told Rita to stay in the truck as he opened the floorboard on the driver's side, grabbed his AK-47 assault rifle and got out of the truck for a better look.

The plane made two passes over the road JJ was hiding on, then banked sharply. As JJ took cover behind a nearby tree, the plane descended and closed to within 100 yards of JJ and Rita's location. In an attempt to gain a better vantage point, JJ ran out into the open toward a briar patch which suddenly became visible under a moonbeam flaring through a passing cloud. The single-engine plane swooped low over JJ's head, knocking him to the ground, then pulled up, banked and went into another dive straight at JJ's moon-lit figure. As he prepared to fire in full automatic mode, the fast approaching Piper suddenly leveled off, throttled back and softly landed in an open field 50 yards short of JJ's firing position.

As the plane's engine died, the door slowly opened and two figures emerged. JJ, already locked and loaded, took aim then caught his breath as he heard a familiar voice call out, "Hey big brother, what's up?" As stunned as a deer in headlights, JJ slowly rose as Curtis walked toward him, followed closely by the plane's pilot. JJ rushed to meet them.

"Curtis!" he called out, then paused and haltingly uttered, "Frank?! You flew this thing?"

"Some of us aeronautical engineers know more than just the *theory* of flight," big Frank Kazmarczyk replied, as he reached out to shake JJ's hand.

"How'd you guys pull this off?" asked JJ. "Well, when we heard dad's plan hit a snag, we went to Plan B. I called old man Byers and asked him if we could use the Piper trainer from his flying school to help you out and he said absolutely, just remember to fill her up."

"Curtis knew I was a pilot," Frank elaborated, "and when he told me your situation and said you were an innocent man, I said *let's go!* And here we are."

"So, what are we waiting for? Let's fly away!" responded a voice from behind them as everyone turned to see Rita stand up, drop the 450 Magnum and extend her arms out from her side, ready to fly free as a bird.

CHAPTER 11

OVER 50 PEOPLE HAD GATHERED on the front lawn. They jockeyed for a good vantage point to see and cheer the returning heroes, who had just survived an engagement with superior forces without suffering a single scratch, casualty or arrest.

The onlookers made way for the trio of vehicles as they slowly stopped in front of the house and the door of the first car opened. After spending an hour of thankful prayer at church, JJ and Rita were spiritually refreshed as they emerged, waving and smiling back at their good friends and neighbors. As they made their way past the well-wishers' *Welcome Home* sign, flanked by two yellow Gadsden flags snapping smartly in the summer breeze, a second cheer went up for the arrival of the rescue team of Curtis and Frank – followed closely by Emma, Jillian, Jeb and Jenny Moultrie and her parents, who were doing their best to keep up with little Camilla as she skipped merrily along to the beat of a song that one of the greeters started to play on his boom box:

> *"Texas, dear Texas, from tyrant grip now free,*
> *Shines forth in splendor, your star of destiny,*
> *Mother of heroes, welcome your children true,*
> *Proclaiming our allegiance, our faith, our love for you.*
> *God bless you, Texas, and keep you brave and strong,*

That you may grow in power and worth, throughout the ages long." *

One by one, the assembled Gadsden flag wavers joined in singing the national anthem of the Republic of Texas until the Moultrie family waved good-bye and disappeared into their home.

Inside the house, streamers were streaming from one corner to another across the ceiling, a 2x4-foot blowup of JJ and Rita behind a "Welcome Home" sash stood on an easel by the bay window and mini Lone Star and Gadsden flags dangled from the crystal chandelier. Hugs and kisses were exchanged throughout the dining room as they all settled into their usual chairs around the more-festive-than-usual table and began to pray.

"Dear Lord," Jeb began, "we thank you for helping our family survive what no member of your flock should have to experience. Thank you for giving JJ the strength to stand up to those who mock the sanctity of life. Thank you for giving Rita the wisdom to see the error of her ways, and thank you for giving Curtis and Frank the means to right what would have been a grievous wrong. A-men."

"Praise the Lord and pass the grits and gravy," JJ called out.

"Now, don't go making light of things, JJ!" scolded Jenny.

"I don't mean no disrespect, mom. I'm just a happy camper, praising the Lord and strengthening my soul with the finest table of down-home cookin' I ever did see! I propose a toast! To mom and dad for holdin' it all together during perilous times; to Rita for believing in me; and to Curtis and Frank, the greatest dynamic duo since Batman and Robin!" The *Cheers!* resounded throughout the room as JJ nodded to mom and dad, winked at Rita, saluted Frank and elbowed Curtis with more affection than he ever realized he possessed.

Before dinner was served, Emma had excused herself so she could run home next door to get the dessert she had made plus one other surprise. Two minutes later, all eyes were on the proudly presented pecan pie Emma learned to make from Jenny and then shifted to the surprise that followed Emma into the room - Maria Estrada.

Emma brought in another chair and set a place at the table for Maria,

---

* <u>Texas, Our Texas</u> - Lyrics by Marsh and Gladys Yoakum Wright; music by William Marsh right next to Camilla. Everyone in the Moultrie household knew that Frank and Emma had taken Maria in, saving her from deportation to Mexico along with her parents, Hector and Juanita, an action that was taken by McCall's Militia under Jeb's command. At the time, Maria was distraught and didn't understand any of it. Emma did her best to explain everything to Maria after class, telling her that her parents had to return to their home country for awhile and that they wanted Maria to stay with her and Frank. This was a possibility that Frank and Emma had discussed at length, knowing that Maria's parents were undocumented, and that if and when the day came they could either look the other way or look the Estradas in the eye and offer a helping hand. They were glad they had chosen the latter.

Since the incident had taken place only a week earlier, no one in the Moultrie home had ever met Maria, who was now overwhelmed by the sea of new faces before her. Emma slowly introduced Maria to everyone at the table starting with the youngest one. Camilla told Maria she liked her pink shoes and that she would read her "Cat got your Tongue?" book to her after dinner.

JJ and Curtis introduced themselves. "I'm JJ, Camilla's big brother. She comes to me whenever somebody tries to pick on her."

"I can take care of myself, JJ!" clarified Camilla.

"I'm Curtis, Camilla's other brother. I'm the smart one. She likes me best."

"Say what!" exclaimed JJ, giving Curtis a shot in the arm.

"Don't pay any attention to them, Maria," advised Rita. "You know how silly boys are!"

"I'm JJ's friend, Rita, and this is Curtis's friend, Jillian." "Hello," said Maria, managing a quiet smile. "And this is Mr. and Mrs. Moultrie," explained Jillian. Maria nodded as her little smile turned upside down at the thought of her own far-away parents. Jeb Moultrie struggled making eye contact with Maria as he managed an uncomfortable "Hello," followed by Jenny's ambivalent, "Yes, hello." Jenny's parents nodded stiffly, uncertain of what to say to the interloper in their midst, as everyone self-consciously reverted to their previous conversations, hoping to rekindle the celebratory tone, but not quite succeeding.

Maria fixed her plate with the help of Jillian and Camilla, as everyone's thoughts returned to recent events. "It was a horrible sight," recounted Rita. "The explosion, the flying glass, the flames. I sure hope they find out who did it."

"Yeah, me too," added JJ. "Pass the chickpeas."

"I couldn't believe the Army they had assembled at the border crossing on old Highway 377," recalled Jeb. "My best Militia man, Zeke, said he could pick off a couple of them to create a diversion, which I put the kibosh on in a hurry. You tryin' to start a war?" I asked him.

"I've been flying since I was 15. That's why I got into aeronautical engineering," explained Frank.

"He put that plane through its paces – my stomach is still churning," acknowledged Curtis.

"You'd have thought Curtis never saw a woman holding a 450 Magnum before," laughed Rita.

"Finally they called me! I'm sitting there at the front line with my Smith & Wesson in my hand and they're flying home. Why am I always the last one to know?" complained Jeb.

The rising cacophony almost drowned out the doorbell, but Camilla heard it, went to the front door, opened it and returned with a message. "Mom, there's someone at the front door," announced Camilla.

"Who is it Camilla, honey" asked Jenny, "one of the neighbors?"

"It's Kay."

"Kay? We don't know any Kay," advised mom.

Camilla explained, "She's an in-guess-ti vate…in gate ive…"

"You mean *investigative*" asked Curtis, recalling a TV talking head he had hoped to forget.

"Yeah. Kay Bailey, in-ves-ti-ga-tive reporter."

The room fell silent as a church mouse, as JJ quickly got up from the table and said, "I'll handle this."

CHAPTER 12

"SO, WHEN WERE YOU GOING to tell me?" asked a smoldering Jillian.

"Tell you what, Jilly?" replied an evasive Curtis.

"What everybody in your family knows but me! You're going away to college!"

"Oh, right. I was going to tell you last week, but you know how crazy everything got, Jill."

"I thought we were going to South Texas State - together!" reminded Jillian.

"I thought so, too, but then I decided to apply to Kilmer's Journalism School as a long shot. My grades are good. I wrote a lot of strong stories and editorials for our school newspaper. Then I had the brainstorm of writing an essay about how journalism is changing here in Texas. I called it The Fate of Journalism in the New Republic. They must have liked it and seen some potential. My tuition is covered, but I'll have to get a job to pay for my room and board."

"What about our potential, Curtis?" questioned Jillian. "What happens to us? My parents can't afford to send me to Kilmer."

"Nothing will change between us, Jillian. We'll talk to each other every day - we'll see new things, meet new people."

"That's what I mean. What if you meet someone else?"

"Nah. Could never happen," promised Curtis. "I'm the one who should be worried about *you!* Those South Texas State Bulldogs can get pretty rambunctious tracking down someone as special as you are!"

"Just remember where you came from and who's waiting for you at home," Jillian tearfully replied as she took Curtis' hand and placed it over her heart.

As if by magic, the chemistry between the two ignited and bubbled up again, overwhelming their senses and overflowing all boundaries. They exchanged kisses, gazes, smiles and tears as they held each other tightly, lovingly, longingly, shutting out the world around them, until the world around them could be shut out no more.

Curtis spent the rest of the summer trying to make as much money as he could to pay for his room, board and books when he enrolled at Kilmer College. Fortunately, he didn't have to look too hard to find a job. JJ was more than happy to help out his little brother and pay back some of the debt he owed for getting him out of that tough spot up in Oklahoma.

His landscaping business was doing better than ever, perhaps because everyone suddenly knew JJ better. By the same token, Curtis was more than happy to indulge in some physical labor that would benefit both JJ and himself. This turned into a full-time summer job for Curtis, as JJ found himself preoccupied with other issues such as his duties with the Militia plus his standoffs with Kay Bailey and the FBI regarding the Oklahoma abortion clinic bombing.

Kay Bailey had become a persistent presence in JJ Moultrie's life. Since the day he slammed the door in her face, she began interviewing his neighbors. "So, how long have you known JJ?"

"All my life," replied a long-time friend. "He's a good man. A devout Christian who would do anything for you."

"How about his girlfriend Rita?" Kay followed up, "would he do anything for her, too?"

"I suppose so. Who wouldn't? He loved that little girl."

"Mrs. Littleton, do you think JJ would take the law into his own hands?"

"JJ's a good Christian," she answered. "He knows right from wrong. And he knows that abortion is murder!"

Another woman identified on the TV screen as a neighbor said, "JJ is welcome at our house anytime. We all love JJ."

A man identified as Zeke Hogan of McCall's Militia added, "We have every right to protect our citizens from illegal abortions. And we're going to do it, too!"

Kay Bailey turned to the TV camera and summarized. "So far, JJ Moultrie has refused our interview requests about the bombing. The receptionist at the Bessler abortion clinic was killed in the explosion, which makes this a United States federal murder investigation. The FBI is still in the process of collecting and analyzing evidence and will be pursuing all legal avenues in order to question Mr. Moultrie. I am told this includes extradition from the Republic of Texas to Oklahoma City. Stay tuned for further details. This is Kay Bailey, KXOTV, Sugarfield, Texas."

Turning off the TV, the Moultries weren't sure whether their neighbors were helping or hurting JJ's cause. However it might be expressed, the court of public opinion was definitely on JJ's side in Sugarfield, and the news media across the Republic remained positive as well. How far the FBI was prepared to go was another question.

The Republic of Texas was a sovereign nation. It didn't answer to the United States of America. Entry could be denied. Extradition could be denied. Protection could be provided. Everyone in the Moultrie household, around the neighborhood and across the Republic sensed a fight was brewing. And if a fight is what they wanted, a fight is what they would get.

CHAPTER 13

KILMER COLLEGE IS A PRESTIGIOUS private school in a pristine setting on Lake Michigan, just north of Chicago in Evanston, Illinois. Its School of Journalism is well respected throughout America and the world, and draws students from everywhere.

People who major in journalism have a desire to delve into human interest stories and communicate them in a compelling manner. They have their finger on the pulse of the public and feel obligated to keep them informed. They are also idealistic people, as most students are. They want to uncover the truth. Right wrongs. Challenge hypocrisy. And cut to the chase.

The overarching national cause that had so many students questioning everything at this time was the relatively recent separation of Texas from the United States of America. Yes, the majority of Texans wanted to leave the union because they felt their values were being undermined by the federal government and that it no longer represented them. Yes, they submitted the required petition to the U.S. government to do so. Yes, separation was granted by the United States Supreme Court because of an obscure law that required any annexation of a sovereign nation, which Texas was at the time, to be affirmed by a two-thirds vote of Congress, which was never taken. Even so, the Court ruled, the Declaration of Independence does give the people the right to "*institute new government*" as they see fit. The quote the court identified states: "*Governments are instituted among men, deriving their powers from the consent of the governed, that whenever any form of government becomes destructive of these ends, it is the right of the people to alter or abolish it, and institute new government.*" And yes, millions of Americans didn't seem to care one way or the other, in much the same sense that millions of Americans never bother to vote.

Nevertheless, this form of secession seemed wrong to those citizens who were paying attention and who were worried about the consequences, especially the younger generation. With their idealism in tow, the journalism students at Kilmer College felt the need to speak out, not just against secession per se, but against two additional problems that had been exacerbated by granting Texas its sovereignty; abortion and immigration. Anti-abortion violence was increasing in America and immigration tensions were heightening at the Mexican border. These were subjects of great debate among college students across the country, and very much so at KC.

Twice a week after class, journalism major Amber Jones led a discussion group of undergraduates in her dorm. An attractive, soft-spoken African American woman with a radiant smile, facile mind and engaging personality, Amber was an easy person to talk to and connect with. Her natural charisma was effervescent and welcoming. When Amber spoke, others listened. She was a natural leader in every way. Dayquan Thomas, also of African American descent, was almost always at Amber's side. Amber and Dayquan had gone to high school together in Kalamazoo, Michigan and were peas in a pod when it came to their ideas of social equality and justice for all. They took the same classes together and they studied together.

The rest of Amber's entourage looked like the United Nations: Omar was from Pakistan; Soon-Lee was from China; Indira was from Calcutta; Vince was Italian American; Wayne and Al were second-generation German Americans and Ken and Joan's grandparents came from Czechoslovakia. The one thing this august group didn't have was a representative from the deep south, which was rectified when a new freshman in a checkered shirt, blue jeans and silver-tipped belt buckle stopped by one evening to say hello to the group he had heard so much about.

Curtis Moultrie was welcomed with open arms because he was cut from the same cloth, shared the pecan pie his mom sent every week and had an insider's perspective on the Republic of Texas.

"Everyone in Texas feels like they are family," Curtis explained. "While everyone is kind of spread out, people still look after one another. There's a lot of history, tradition, independence and family values all wrapped up into one."

"Sounds very homey, Curtis," volunteered Indira. "The country of my birth has very strong family ties, too." "As does mine," seconded Omar. "How do you say it here…we are all in this together."

"Which begs the question…" interjected Vince in his usual pointed manner…"what were you thinking when you seceded from the United States?"

"First of all, Vince, it wasn't secession. We always were a sovereign nation and that requires a different level of annexation which never occurred. Texas isn't like any other state."

"You got that right….partner," Vince not-so-tactfully agreed.

"Plus," Curtis went on, "the issue had a lot to do with cultural values. The vast majority of Texans are against abortion, illegal immigrants, gun control, gay marriage. Religion is a factor, too. There are some very strong Christian fundamentalist groups down there that have been calling for actual secession for a long time. Plus, the federal government was getting bigger and bigger, spending more money and passing legislation that was very unpopular in our part of the country. Texas isn't alone in that regard, you know. Other southern states have a similar attitude, and they are kind of waiting and watching to see how things go in our new Republic."

"We are watching, too, Curtis," commented Soon-Lee. We think it would be sad if the United States broke up the way some other countries have. The United States must continue to be a leader in the free world. Must continue to be strong. Must be United!"

"I don't disagree with you, Soon-Lee," replied Curtis. "In my heart of hearts, I liked it the way it was. But most of my family doesn't. They felt they were losing their freedom, and their values were being ignored. Family comes first, doesn't it?"

"Speaking of family…"interjected Vince, as a light bulb went off in his head, "are you related to that other Moultrie…the one who bombed the abortion clinic?"

"JJ is my brother, but he didn't have anything to do with the bombing," Curtis snapped back.

"But you rescued him, didn't you?" Vince followed up.

"Wouldn't you, if your brother was in some sort of trouble?" Curtis replied, feeling his temperature rising and his composure falling.

"Alright folks," interceded Amber, "I think that's enough of the third degree. Clearly, Curtis has the same desire that we do to live in harmony with one another and to spread the word however we can. He's been sort of caught between a rock and a hard place in Texas. I think that's why he's here."

"Hey, Curtis, welcome to the club!" Wayne chimed in, extending his hand in brotherhood. "We all want to see some changes made."

"Don't feel like the Lone Ranger," Dayquan advised. "Debate is healthy. Debate is what we want!"

"Nothing personal, Curtis," Vince chimed in. "I just get frustrated sometimes trying to express myself."

"No problem," replied Curtis, as the group formally welcomed the man from the Lone-Star-State-turned Republic and eagerly gathered around the pecan pie.

From the back of the room, Amber surveyed her principled contemporaries and felt the renewed electricity provided by Curtis Moultrie. And it felt good.

CHAPTER 14

SAYING CURTIS' CLASSES AT KILMER were difficult was like saying there was once a little trouble at the Alamo. He immediately realized he would have to spend the majority of his days and nights studying. Everything. This was in addition to his duties as a waiter at Tony's Ribs which helped pay for his room and board.

Then there were Amber's bi-weekly meetings with her engaging, inspiring group. They had so much to talk about and so much to do, it was all Curtis could do to keep his mind on his books. And yet the idea of "all work and no play" didn't seem right either. Especially after he got to know Amber better. And vice versa. They had a lot in common. Their viewpoints were so similar they could almost read each other's minds. They were on the same wavelength, and the message was coming through loud and clear.

After one solid month of studying, cramming, waiting on tables, meeting with the group, calling mom and saying he was fine, and calling Jillian and saying he missed her, Curtis was ready for a break. The opportunity presented itself after another group meeting ended and Amber approached Curtis with some personal questions. "So, what do you like to do for fun, Curtis?"

"I like...Ferris Wheels" replied Curtis, surprising himself with the originality of his reply.

"Really?" responded a quizzical Amber.

"When we have our county fairs, I like to ride the Ferris Wheel," explained Curtis. "It's a big one, 40-feet high! I also like mustangs."

"Oh? Of course you like to ride horses, too. You're from Texas!"

"Amber, please. I'm no cowboy just because I wear a cowboy hat sometimes."

"I kind of like it, Curtis. It suits you! Do you wear leather pants, too?"

"Leather pants? You mean chaps?"

"Yeah, chaps. And six-shooters. Do you have six-shooters, Curtis?"

"Amber, I don't have gun fights, and I don't round up horses. That mustang I mentioned is my candy-apple red 1973 Mustang convertible."

"Oh, that kind of mustang!"

"Right. It's a V-8 with Holly Carb and posi-traction rear end."

"I'm sure I don't know what any of that means, but…."

"Well I'd be glad to clear it all up for you, Amber. Want to go for a ride tonight?" asked an obviously smitten Curtis.

"Yes, I would," Amber haltingly replied.

"Maybe you could show this *country boy* around," goaded Curtis.

"I know just the place," replied an obviously smitten Amber.

Curtis dropped the top on his newly washed and detailed Mustang and picked up Amber at her dorm at 7 PM, ready to follow her lead in more ways than one. As Amber settled into her seat, Curtis announced "Pilot to Navigator, chart our course, please."

"Navigator to Pilot…take Sheridan Road to Lake Shore Drive, and head due south."

"South to what?" inquired the Pilot.

"You'll know it when you see it," communicated the Navigator.

A few minutes later, Curtis turned onto "The Drive" and glanced over to see Lake Michigan on his left, green parks and elegant condos on his right, a million stars overhead and the beautiful city of broad shoulders arrayed across his windshield.

Amber inserted a disc into the CD player, gave Curtis a quick glance, sat back in her seat and listened to the beat of the city:

"There's a road I'd like to tell you about, it lives in my hometown,
Lake Shore Drive the road is called, and it'll take you up or down

from rags on up to riches, fifteen minutes you can fly,
pretty blue lights along the way, help you ride on by,
and the blue light's shinin' with a heavenly grace, help you ride on by.
There ain't no road just like it, anywhere I've found,
runnin' south on Lake Shore Drive, headin' into town
just slippin' on by on LSD, Friday night trouble bound." **

As the miles drifted by, Curtis felt himself engulfed in a mesmerizing new world of star-studded attractions. The dazzling hi-rise condominiums, "pretty blue lights" of office towers and cooling, fresh-water breezes clearly indicated he was not in Sugarfield anymore. Curtis snapped out of his reverie, turned to a dreamy-eyed Amber and asked, "Are we there yet?"

"Take the Oak Street Exit to Michigan Avenue and follow the bright lights," directed the Navigator, with a knowing smile.

Curtis merged onto the "Mag Mile," a glorious stretch of Michigan Avenue that showcased the glittery storefronts of Tiffany, Cartier, Ralph Lauren, Sak's Fifth Ave and others, sharing prime real estate space with the old Chicago Water Tower, the only public building that survived the great Chicago fire of 1871. Curtis reined in his trusty Mustang as he maneuvered his way around the tourist-laden horse and buggy carriages that plied The Avenue, then turned to Amber and said, "This is all amazingly cool, but way beyond my pay grade. Is this what you wanted to show me? You said you knew *just the place!"*

"Turn left on Grand Avenue," directed Amber. Curtis did as he was told, and by his dead reckoning, was now headed due east which confused him even more. Chicago has no east side, except for a few blocks. That's where the lake comes in. And that's when Curtis saw it: Navy Pier…and its huge, colossal, magnificent Ferris Wheel. Awash and aglow in a million flickering lights, the slowly turning super-sized wheel was filled to capacity with heaven-sent, starry-eyed souls.

Curtis turned to Amber and simply said, "I love it!"

"I knew you would," replied a giddy Amber, as Curtis pulled into the parking lot. The two of them popped out of the car and raced for the entrance to The Pier like a couple of kids, pointing and grinning in affirmation at the fun sights and sounds that greeted them inside. Curtis led the way past the

---

** Lake Shore Drive by Aliotta, Haynes and Jeremiah

open-air restaurants, vendors, souvenirs and boat tour promoters to the foot of the wheel that had to be considered *gigantic*, even by Texas standards.

When their turn came, Curtis doffed his invisible cowboy hat, bowed and proclaimed, "After you, my lady!"

"Gallantry will get you everywhere," responded Amber, as she performed a graceful curtsy. The normally nonchalant ticket taker was so impressed with the twosome's theatrics that he closed the cabin door behind them with a spectacularly dramatic flourish.

"Going up," observed an eager Curtis.

"As you wish, Sir Gallahad," replied Amber, still in full character.

"You are taking me to new heights, Miss Jones," Curtis countered.

"That was my plan, Sir Moultrie." The massive wheel continued its upward trek, occasionally stopping for new passengers along the way, each time affording a view of the city that was more spectacular than the last. By the time it reached its pinnacle, Curtis and Amber had ceased the snappy dialogue and were quietly enjoying the moment together, side-by-side.

"I love the quiet," whispered Amber.

"I love the view," countered Curtis, turning toward Amber to make his point. They reached for each other's hand, found each other's soul and exchanged kisses as gently as snowflakes fall. The ride down to the ground was as silent as the ride up was boisterous. Curtis and Amber had connected in that special way in which pure emotions are touched, excited and intermingled into a feeling of oneness. Never to be undone again.

The rest of the evening included dinner on the Pier at the Billy Goat Tavern, the iconic restaurant known for the curse that was put on the Chicago Cubs by the restaurant's owner for not allowing admittance to Wrigley Field of himself - *and his goat* - many years earlier. As curses go, this was a good one, inasmuch as the Cubs have still not won a World Series since 1907. Curtis and Amber topped off dinner with a ride on the Pier's carousel, which provoked peals of laughter from Amber and a more melancholy reaction from Curtis as his thoughts returned to the Ft. Bend County stag he had ridden months earlier and to the promise he had made to his faithful companion, Jillian.

The leisurely drive back to the Kilmer campus was quietly exciting for both riders, as they sang the song of Lake Shore Drive in unison while firmly holding hands in the candy apple red convertible.

CHAPTER 15

THE PRESIDENTIAL SEAL FILLED THE TV screen as an off-camera voice intoned, "Ladies and gentlemen, the President of the Republic of Texas." The camera pulled back and tilted up revealing Pres. Jefferson McCall in a dark blue suit, embroidered white shirt with pearl snaps and Windsor-knotted red and blue tie with one single star in the center, sitting behind a desk flanked by the yellow Gadsden flag on his right and the Lone-Star flag on his left. His welcoming manner lasted all of twenty seconds after which his countenance turned grim and decisive.

"My fellow citizens of the great Republic of Texas, I thank you for welcoming me into your homes this evening to give you a brief update of recent events concerning incidents at our northern and southern borders. As you know, our borders extend for over 3,000 miles all around the great Republic of Texas, including 1,000 at the border with Mexico. They are as proper and true as the fence you may have surrounding your ranch, your property, your yard. Borders are there for your protection – to keep out what you want to keep out and to keep in what you want to keep in. Borders are not to be trifled with. Yours or ours. Crossing them requires permission. Any attempt to cross them without permission should be met with swift and strict opposition. This applies to our northern borders where entry has been threatened by foreign law enforcement agencies in pursuit of persons of interest in our Republic regarding violent acts committed in the state of Oklahoma. These law enforcement agencies have no jurisdiction here and they will be turned away as a matter of course. The persons they seek maintain their innocence and will not be extradited to the United States to stand trial in a court of law that is prejudiced against our beliefs, our values and our way of life.

By the same token, the borders to our south are being threatened by outsiders as well, and they, too, will be turned away by any and all means necessary. Furthermore, we shall continue to round up and deport all illegal aliens, and we are increasing our border patrols in order to stem the continuing incursions into our land. By executive order I am requiring the militia to assume a greater role in keeping the Republic safe by extending their tours of duty. I ask for your understanding and your cooperation as we increase the scope and duration of your family members' responsibilities. We must fight for what we have always fought for: freedom. When our borders are secure, our lives are secure. There is no turning back. Not now. Not ever. Thank you, God bless you and God bless the last bastion of freedom in the northern hemisphere: the Republic of Texas."

As the TV screen returned to regularly scheduled programming, a downcast Jenny asked, "So, Jeb dear, you will be leaving us?"

Jeb turned off the TV with his remote control from the head of the table and replied, "Yes, for a while. But, it's not like I've got a lot of work to do here anyway. There's not much construction going on these days, as we all know."

"Oh, we'll be alright, Jeb," comforted Jenny, "I'm just worried about you."

"It's not a big deal," reassured Jeb. "There are some remote outposts that need shoring up, that's all. We're just going to have to get tougher. I'm not taking JJ though. He can stay home."

"Well, I'm grateful for that, Jeb. But it still sounds dangerous."

"Roping a steer is dangerous, Jenny dear, unless you know what you're doing."

"Mom," JJ chimed in, "dad's the best. He's a great leader and a great shot."

"Woah, were not talking about shooting anybody here. This is just a show of force to let them know what they're up against. They'll run off into the sunset the minute we show up in our Humvees. They're just unorganized rabble in broken down trucks and on foot. They'll get the message. Besides, I'll have Zeke riding shotgun with me."

"Just don't start something you can't finish is all I'm saying," offered Jenny.

"And when was that ever the case, Jenny my love?" reminded Jeb as he gave Jenny an extended peck on the cheek.

"Easy son," mother Taylor advised. "Remember your blood pressure!"

When the grins and muffled laughter subsided Jenny retracted her objections, father Taylor shouted out "Stand your ground," JJ served dad another wedge of key lime pie, and Camilla sadly looked over at the empty chair next to her and wondered what Curtis would have done.

CHAPTER 16

CAPT. JEB MOULTRIE PUT ON his camouflage fatigues, military boots and pill box cap and met "Shotgun" Zeke and six other members of his squad at the Houston Motor Pool to get vehicles for their tour of duty along the Mexican border. Jeb requisitioned one Republic of Texas Humvee for himself and Zeke, and three more for the rest of his command. These high-mobility, multipurpose war vehicles (HMMWV) are diesel powered four-wheel-drive tactical trucks designed to carry sophisticated communications and weapons systems. The hand-lettered motto on the side of Jeb's Humvee – "Don't Mess with Texas" – said it all.

Seeing a convoy of these bad boys on the highways and byways of any locality was a source of true "Shock and Awe." On this day they were given a wide berth by every passenger car they passed along Highway 77 en route to Falfurrias, Texas, Capt. Moultrie's first stop. It was here that Junior Bostick, Chief Deputy of the Brooks County Sheriff's office had reported a significant increase in illegal immigration.

He was one happy lawman when he heard the militia rumble into his town in their Humvees. As he set out some folding chairs and a plate of bear claws in his small office, the Chief reported, "It's out of control Capt. Moultrie. They're coming up through the Rio Grande Valley. We've got checkpoints at Mission and at Pharr on Highway 281 but they're still getting through. We catch a few stumbling around the plains, but a lot of them are more organized. They've got vehicles. Some are runnin' drugs. Some have heavy weapons!"

"Well, we're here to discourage that kind of behavior Chief," Capt. Moultrie replied. "By the time you see a problem up here, the cat's already out of the bag. We've got to get to the source: the Rio Grande. That's where they're coming across by rubber dingy, speed boat and dog paddle."

"We've got some big fences down there Capt." the chief advised.

"Yes, we do Chief Bostic, but some are bigger than others and none of them are big enough, and that's what our construction crews are working on right now. Until then, myself and the rest the militia will be providing cover."

"I'd like to give them a warning shot across the bow. That would keep their heads down for a long time, if not for good!" interjected Zeke. "You keep that itchy trigger finger on your bear claw, Shotgun. Our orders are to present *A Show of Force* to the undocumented and the unwelcome. I repeat: A...Show...of force!

We will be running regular patrols up and down Highway 83 from Brownsville to Laredo while our boys build our fences higher, stronger and longer. Other militia units will be making similar runs from Laredo to Del Rio and from Del Rio to El Paso at the Arizona and New Mexico borders. Let's stay in touch, Chief. Thanks for the input and for the hospitality."

The two officers shook hands, then saluted as Capt. Jeb Moultrie fired up his turbocharged V-8 behemoth, then fired up his men with the best John Wayne impression he could muster: "Saddle up, men. Remember the Alamo!"

The immigration problem in the Republic of Texas is a complex one. Every year thousands of Mexican and Central American refugees attempt to flee crime, violence and poverty by illegally entering the United States or trespassing across the soft underbelly of the Republic of Texas.

The money alone is worth the risk. The average salary for a construction worker in Mexico is six dollars per day, if any jobs are even available. Working in a grocery store could pay five dollars a day. Selling bottled water on the street may bring three dollars for the entire day. Meanwhile, just across the Rio Grande a man can earn five dollars *an hour* bussing tables in a restaurant, picking fruit in an orchard, mowing lawns in someone's yard.

This is the same kind of appeal that lured millions of immigrants to America's shores over 250 years ago. However, when those "huddled masses" steamed into US waters en masse, they were all funneled through Ellis Island; one point of entry for one boatload of people. Trying to oversee 18 official and numerous unofficial entry points along the Rio Grande is a different story altogether.

The Republic of Texas' version of a Chinese Wall is a hodgepodge of sections of 10-foot walls with video cameras on top, scattered barbed wire fences and simple vehicle barricades that run alongside the highways. It is still a work in progress, and a lot of undocumented immigrants have already slipped through. Closing the door after the horses have left the barn is *Immigration Problem Number One.*

There are currently an estimated one million undocumented immigrants at work or at large in the Republic of Texas. Some have become a low-cost workforce which is of benefit to local ranchers and businessmen, yet they are still as illegal as a boatload of early Europeans who might have run aground off the coast of Coney Island and swum ashore. Once they are identified as "illegals," there is the distinct likelihood that these people will be rounded up and put on the next bus to Mexico just as Jeb Moultrie & Co. did to Hector and Juanita Estrada and others in the recent past. Sending undocumented immigrants home re-starts the vicious cycle of border crossings that often leads to desperate measures and *Immigration Problem Number Two.*

Many recidivist border crossers try again by turning to people who say they will *guarantee* safe crossing *and employment* for themselves and their families - for a price. These immigrant smugglers, known as "coyotes," pack passengers into vans and transport them across the border with bogus papers or passed border agents who had been encouraged to look the other way.

More often than not this approach falls short of expectations, as these coyotes release their passengers in the middle of nowhere in the middle of night, ready to be victimized by yet another coyote, this time the four-legged kind. The large and lonely ranches and rugged terrain of southern Texas is strewn with the evidence of smuggled immigrants who never arrived at their imagined destination. Those who lived to tell their stories, tell them to people like Jeb Moultrie, a scenario he thought he had come upon one night in his Humvee, only to discover that what he had really stumbled across was *Immigration Problem Number Three.*

There is no overestimating the amount of crime and violence that the average Mexican national faces on a daily basis. Drug gangs rule many provincial territories and are constantly at war with one another over control of their turf. This violence spills over into the homes and lives of innocent citizens. What little they may have is taken from them under threat of harm to their family.

Anyone who smuggles illegal aliens, drug runners or sex slaves across the border must also pay a tribute to the gang in their area. If you do not pay the piper, you answer to the "Zetas," a group of enforcers made up of Mexican Army deserters. The more ambitious gangs, Knights Templar and C3, become drug dealers or soldiers for the Mexican Gulf cartels. They become the army that fights its way through skirmishes with the Mexican police, crosses the Mexican border under cover of night or duress and establishes its position in "The Plaza" - their term for the Rio Grande Valley in the Republic of Texas and the established drug network that emanates from it.

In "government-speak," these gangs are referred to as TCOs, or Transnational Criminal Organizations because they come from Mexico, Honduras, Guatemala and El Salvador. Venezuela has also been helping Middle Eastern individuals enter the Republic of Texas through Mexico. They all deal in drugs. By association, they also deal in death.

American citizens as well as Republic of Texas citizens have been killed during run-ins with Mexican drug dealers during recent years, though actionable evidence has been impossible to come by. Citizens of the Republic are also routinely kidnapped along the Mexican border for sex or ransom. Some are never released. Anyone who lives and works along the border is aware of the dangers lurking there, which is why Capt. Jeb Moultrie stayed seated behind his bullet-proof windshield as he forced the banged up delivery van that looked suspicious off the road and ordered it to open up.

It is one thing to stop a van and find a troupe of tired, hungry, unhappy campers inside, yearning to be free but amenable to going home. It is quite another to stop a van and see the doors pop open like the lid of a wind-up music box, and a grinning, leering clown pop out - only this one has automatic weapons. And so does his buddy.

It happened fast. As the side door of the van flew open, Jeb caught a quick glimpse of tightly wrapped bricks of pure white powder before a flash of light from the blue steel barrel of an AK-47 sent a hundred screaming messages of instant doom at his highly fortified, heavy metal cocoon. Instinct and adrenalin, every soldier's friend, took over and spun the Humvee away from the firepower and into a doughnut slide now aiming directly at the side of the fire-breathing van.

The van lurched forward, as the hard-charging Humvee just clipped its rear bumper. Whoever was driving that van had dropped a new engine into its bay and was now crackin' the whip over 400 horses, minimum. When the van zigged, Jeb zigged. When the van turned on a dime, Jeb left five cents change. "JJ and Curtis, you should see me now!" Jeb yelled to the chariots of the gods as Zeke continued peppering the elusive target.

The van made a hard left, directly toward the Rio Grande. "He's making a run for the border," Shotgun screamed over the roar of the Humvee and the bursts of his own AK-47.

"I'm on him Zeke, till Kingdom come," Jeb advised as the van approached an intersection with blinking red lights overhead. The driver floored it and plowed through the intersection, taking out two cars and a pickup truck in the process. The van took a beating, too, but continued speeding ahead down a dirt road toward the river with a bashed-in, broken-down front end, smoke pouring out of the engine and flames shooting out the exhaust.

"Now that looks like the kind of truck those Mexicans love to show off, Zeke: a custom-built low rider with hydraulic action and hot pink neon underneath. I'm impressed!" observed Jeb as he continued in hot pursuit. A few feet from the Rio Grande, the van spun around and stopped cold. Two men jumped out, each one carrying a large package of shrink-wrapped drugs. They threw themselves and their goods into a rubber dingy that was hidden under a tarp near the shore and shoved off. They fired a few shots at the approaching Humvee, then fired up the outboard motor and headed for open waters.

"Where are you going, Captain?" Zeke yelled again. "You think you can cross over into Mexico in this?"

"What's the matter, Shotgun? Didn't bring your passport? You worried about papers? We don't need no stinkin' papers!" prodded Jeb, in his best Mexican bandito accent, as he laughed all the way to the shoreline, burying the accelerator.

The M1113 Humvee has 60-inch water fording capabilities, and it took to the Rio Grande like a duck takes to water. It was actually gaining ground on the little dingy as the water level rose to the top of its wheel wells. Drug Runner #1 was manning the motor while Drug Runner #2 pulled out a semi-automatic rifle and started popping away at the Humvee-turned-PT Boat. Zeke activated the .50 caliber M2HB Machine Gun, which was standard equipment on this particular model, and blew Drug Runner #2 clean out of the boat. "Nice shootin', Tex!" Jeb remarked as he gave his second officer a big "Thumbs up." "I'm takin #1 myself! When I pull alongside, you take the wheel!" Jeb turned to the right for a better angle, then propelled himself onto the amazed dingy captain in a flurry of fists, kicks and karate chops.

As the boat steered itself south, the fight began. Jeb wasn't as young as he used to be, but he remembered his military training and the moves came back to him in a flash. The drug runner wasn't that great of a threat without a gun in his hand, but he still packed a punch and managed to land a few on Capt. Moultrie. Jeb returned the favor and it was touch and go between the two pugilists for a few minutes until Jeb landed a haymaker squarely on the jaw of his opponent and knocked him head-over-heels into the Rio Grande. Jeb regained his senses and scanned the waters for any sign of his foe. About fifty yards off the starboard side, Jeb picked up the bobbing head and flaying arms of a swimmer heading away from the boat. Before he could turn the dingy around, he practically flew out of the boat himself as it suddenly and violently ran aground.

As Jeb looked around and tried to get his bearings, he was suddenly blinded by an array of searchlights coming from the top of four heavy-duty pickup trucks on the shore. The voice on the bullhorn said: "You have entered Mexico illegally. You are under arrest. Raise your hands and step out of the boat." Capt. Jeb Moultrie shakily stood up, wiped the blood, sweat and grime off his face, looked his captors in the eye and simply said: "Ooops!"

CHAPTER 17

MARIA ESTRADA DIDN'T HAVE MANY friends in the new neighborhood she was living in with the Kazmarczyks. Maria missed her deported parents badly, but she felt comfortable living with Emma and Frank. She was old enough to understand and appreciate what they had done for her, and as they often told her, one day she would be reunited with her parents. This helped Maria concentrate on her classes, which she did with a passion.

Maria continued to excel in science and now had the extra advantage of living with Emma, the infamous evolutionary teacher at Sugarfield Middle School, whom she could go to with questions at any time and get instant answers. Maria studied at home, except when her new good friend asked her over for help with her classes in spelling and arithmetic. Camilla was only in the first grade, but Maria was eager to help in much the same way that Emma had helped her. The usual routine revolved around Maria going next door after dinner to help Camilla study with a pile of homemade S'mores to nibble on.

Maria was very good at explaining addition and subtraction, and the thought crossed her mind that someday she might be a teacher, and follow in the footsteps of such a smart and wonderful person as Emma. Sometimes, Maria would bring her own textbooks to study while Camilla was studying hers. On this particular night, Maria was preparing for her upcoming science exam. The ever-inquisitive Camilla couldn't help but notice the interesting pictures in Maria's science textbook and started asking a lot of questions. "Is that a picture of the bones in your hand Maria?" asked Camilla "They look so tiny."

"Yes, Camilla, it's a very small skeleton of a hand from *2 million years ago*. It was found in South Africa by scientists," answered Maria.

"That little hand is 2 million years old? How can that be?" asked Camilla.

"It can't be, Camilla dear" answered Jenny Moultrie, looking over her daughter's shoulder at Maria's book.

"But it's true, Mrs. Moultrie," countered Maria. "The book says: *this was the most powerful case so far in identifying the transitional figure that came before modern humans. It is strong confirmation of evolutionary theory.*"

"Nonsense, Maria," retorted Jenny. "It says it's only a theory."

"But Mrs. Kazmarczyk says....." Maria began.

"I don't care what Mrs. Kaz-mar-czyk says, Maria. We read the Bible in this house and there's no story of a 2 million-year-old *hand* in that book."

Grandma Taylor, who was visiting her daughter and sitting in the overstuffed armchair next to grandpa Taylor looked up and said, "I think you should leave now, Maria. It's past Camilla's bedtime."

Grandpa firmly nodded his assent, but Camilla insisted "I'm not tired grandma. I didn't even get to read my new book to Maria yet!"

"I'm sorry, dear. Say goodbye to Maria," instructed Jenny.

After a sorrowful pause, Camilla looked at Maria and said, "I have to go to bed now. Thank you for helping me with my arithmetic. I like your book, too."

"Camilla!"… reprimanded Jenny.

"Good night, Camilla," Maria obliged. "I'm glad I could help you. Thank you for the S'mores, Mrs. Moultrie and grandma Taylor. Good night!" Camilla gave Maria a huge hug, Jenny and grandma Taylor nodded their goodbyes and Maria gathered up her books. As Maria was about to leave, the doorbell rang. Jenny opened it and was greeted by the unexpected sight of two senior officers in Militia uniforms who had some information to report: *Capt. Jeb Moultrie was MIA – missing in action, from his patrol at the Mexican border.* As the message hit home,

Jenny dropped what was left of the S'mores, Maria stood frozen in place, Camilla yelled out "Mom!" and grandma Taylor fell back in her chair, grabbed her arm, then her chest as she doubled over in pain from the heart attack.

CHAPTER 18

IF ANYONE WERE TO SET about creating one city that reflected the diverse ethnic, cultural and political backgrounds of the United States of America, that one city would be Evanston, Illinois. On any given day, any number of interesting and diverse individuals can be observed doing business, debating, dining, congregating or enjoying each other's company on the streets of Evanston or cheering for the Kilmer College Wildcats at the football field or basketball arena.

On this particular day, members of the Amber Jones journalism gang were enjoying a low-budget taco dinner at a popular outdoor café on Main Street. Vince was holding court, leading a discussion of current events including the agonizingly slow abortion clinic bombing investigation, the ongoing immigrant deportations and the recent shootings at the Mexican border which was "Breaking News" for all of 24 hours.

"People should not be rounding up other people as though they are cattle," Vince began. "There is no excuse for breaking up families or bombing abortion clinics or firing on people at border crossings. That is what fanatics in Third World countries do. Where is the outrage? Where is the full story?"

"You won't get any arguments at this table, Vince," seconded Joan.

"People are either uninformed or misinformed about what is going on in these places," added Omar. "We should speak out. Speak the truth."

"A lot of it comes from this secession business," offered Dayquan. "Things are getting out of control fast."

"Our professors teach us to do whatever it takes to get the facts," added Soon-Lee. "The 24-hour news cycle only provides superficial coverage. It is here today and gone tomorrow. There is no digging. No depth. How can we do more?"

"Curtis," Vince interjected, "you're from where the action is. You must have some insight into this."

"Like I said before, Vince, people are more focused on how things affect their personal lives down there. The big picture is a lot smaller for them."

"So, what would you do, Curtis," Amber asked. "You know the territory, where would you start?"

Curtis ran the question through his mind. "I don't know offhand, let me think about it. Maybe there is a way."

"Let's all put our heads together and *do something*," Amber went on. "I don't think any of us is interested in coasting through life when we know we can make a difference."

The group felt encouraged after their brainstorming session, and they headed back to the campus with a renewed determination to bring some clarity to a world of fleeting interests and unfounded convictions. At least they were determined to give it the old college try. Ideas were percolating in all of their heads as they returned to their respective dorms.

The Eureka moment for Curtis hit him after he had just served his last order of baby back ribs at Tony's that night. He took off his name tag, tallied up his tips and headed over to Amber's place with an idea that was certain to make her day. She answered the door with a look of surprise that was surpassed only by Curtis' expression of dismay as he looked over her shoulder and saw Dayquan sitting on her bed with a beer in hand.

"Curtis, I wasn't expecting you," admitted Amber.

"Obviously," Curtis replied.

"We were just doing a little last-minute cramming," explained Amber.

"Oh. Is that what we're calling it now?" asked Curtis with a vengeance he didn't know he possessed.

"Curtis! We've got a midterm tomorrow, and we're studying for it. What did you want to see me about?"

"It can wait. I don't want to interrupt… anything." Curtis turned around and walked away from a shaken Amber, not knowing what else she could have said.

Curtis couldn't study, sleep or think so he went for a walk on the nearby beach. He looked to the night sky and listened to his heart for guidance, but none was forthcoming. He had no idea how deeply he felt about Amber. Seeing her that close to someone else was more than he could bear. Maybe this shot in the gut was for the best. Now he could focus his energies on the reason he came here in the first place: to learn how to make human contact via the written word. It would be his job to enlighten people and encourage them to think and care and play an active role in the world around them.

A writer could do that, Curtis thought. A writer could make people feel things they had never felt before; see things they had never seen before. And yet, connecting with people is a two-way street. The response may not be commensurate with the stimulus. The feelings have to be reciprocal.

Curtis had just about convinced himself that things turn out for the best, as his mother had so often said, when he absentmindedly bumped into another lost soul on the shore of Lake Michigan. He immediately offered his apology to the silhouetted figure before him who simply replied, "No apologies necessary, Curtis. I was looking for you."

Amber opened her arms to the unsuspecting beachcomber, who hesitated for a moment, then grasped the opportunity with all his might. After being locked in a maddeningly warm embrace, they separated and Amber spread out the oversized blanket she had brought with her. They made themselves comfortable on the shifting sands, and the two journalism students finally got around to communicating with each other.

"Why did you run away from my room?" Amber wanted to know.

"Because, well…you and Dayquan were always together and then when I saw him in your room - on your bed - I guess that was the final straw," he rambled.

"Curtis," Amber explained, getting as close to him as the pages in a book, "Dayquan…is…gay."

"Gay?" replied a dumbfounded Curtis. "As in…*gay?* he repeated.

"Out and proud!" reaffirmed Amber. "I thought you knew."

"I know now and I'm darned happy for him! Not that there's anything wrong with that!"

"Nothing at all!" seconded Amber.

"Nada!" confirmed Curtis.

"Nil!" concluded Amber.

When they eventually ran out of synonyms, they got around to sealing their agreement with a kiss, a hug and a roll in the sand until they closed their eyes in mental and physical exhaustion and didn't open them again until Amber saw the sunlight filtering through the blanket that covered them like a couple of beached baby belugas. "It's 6 o'clock! I've got a test in two hours!" exclaimed a horrified Amber

"Holy mackerel!" offered Curtis. "Is that what I smell by the way, or are they not freshwater fish?"

"This is no joke Curtis. I've got to go. By the way, what did you want to talk to me about last night?" Amber asked as she re-arranged her clothes and hair.

"I've got a way to get to the bottom of the story we want to tell. I just have to make a phone call."

"Then do it! See you later!"

Curtis pulled his cell phone out of his pocket to check his messages and discovered it was dead. No news is good news, right? He got up, brushed himself off and headed to his dorm to make a very important call. He needed to talk to the one person who could help him get the story everybody wanted to tell. He needed to talk to his dad.

CHAPTER 19

CURTIS TOOK THE NEXT FLIGHT home. He left a message for Amber that his father was missing in action on the Mexican border and that his grandmother had a heart attack when she heard about it. He said he would be in touch when he had more information.

JJ picked up Curtis at the airport and filled him in with all the details. Grandma Taylor was recovering from her mild heart attack. No one knew anything about their dad's whereabouts or condition. The three other Humvees in his squad were still making their border runs looking for something – anything – that would give them a clue as to where Capt. Moultrie might be. At the same time, McCall's Militia was formulating a plan that began with a thorough reconstruction of events at the place where he was last heard from and possibly culminate in a fleet of Humvees crossing the border with battle flags flying.

To this point, there had been no information provided by the Mexican border patrol, the Mexican police or the Mexican army. For all intents and purposes, Capt. Jeb Moultrie had disappeared. All official inquiries from the Republic of Texas to the Mexican government had gone unanswered. The Texas National Guard was standing by.

"So what's your plan, JJ?" Curtis wanted to know.

"The plan is we're going to bring him home," JJ answered with conviction.

"What can I do to help?" asked Curtis.

"Just let us do our thing," JJ replied.

"And what would that be if you don't mind my asking?"

"That is classified information, little brother. Some of the best military minds in south Texas are working on it."

"That's what I was afraid of," sparred Curtis. "So you don't need me in this deal?"

"No. You look after mom - and most of all, grandma Taylor. She got through it all like a champ, but is real weak. She needs cheering up, and so does grandpa. Her heart attack affected him, too. He's kind of out of it, kind of delirious."

"Alright," Curtis replied. "I owe Jillian a conversation, too."

"Yeah, she's been wondering about you Curtis, wondering what's going on up there. What *is* going on up there in *Illinois*, by the way. Do you like it?"

"I like it, JJ," Curtis answered, knowing full well it was a far more complicated situation than he could describe. "I like it a lot!"

"Good," JJ replied. "I thought you might amount to something someday. Now, you do your thing and I'll do mine," JJ ordered as they headed up the stairs to their front door totally in unison.

The house Curtis entered didn't feel anything like the home he had left just a few short months ago. He was greeted with smiles and hugs from his mom and Camilla, but the atmosphere was as solemn and dour as a funeral. His mother looked drawn and weary, and she was constantly dabbing at her sniffly nose with her handkerchief. "How are you doing mom? Curtis asked ever-so sweetly. Holding up okay? I hear grandma is good, and a lot of people are working hard to bring dad home."

"Curtis, it's so good to see you," Jenny responded, managing a wan smile. "Yes, I'll be okay. It's just that everything happened so fast. Are you hungry?"

"No, I'm not, mom. Can I get *you* anything?" asked Curtis.

"No, dear, just come with me to see grandma at the hospital. She'll be happy to see you."

Jenny and her children arrived at the hospital in less than a half hour.

Grandma Taylor was in her room in a hospital bed, breathing evenly but heavily, eyes closed. Grandpa Taylor was at her side with his head down, holding her hand through the hospital bed bars, eyes closed. Curtis leaned over the bed and said, "Hi grandma! It's Curtis. How are you feeling?"

Grandma Taylor stirred, her eyes fluttered open and a smile creased her tired face as she looked up at her handsome grandson. "I've had better days, Curtis," she managed to reply with a nod of her head.

"You'll be fine, grandma. You just need to get your strength back," reassured Curtis.

"I know, I know," grandma replied with a sigh.

"And how are you doing, grandpa? You look good!"

"Give 'em hell, boys! Give it to 'em good!" grandpa Taylor ordered.

Curtis felt Camilla tug at his sleeve and he bent down to comfort her. "Camilla honey, Grandma is feeling better. She's going to be okay."

"I know," she tearfully nodded. "But where is daddy? Are you going to bring him home?"

"Yes we are," whispered Curtis, as he led her away from the hospital bed. "JJ and Mr. Kaczmaczyk and the militia men know what to do."

"I want everything to be the way it was," Camilla pleaded. "Not like this. I don't like this."

"I know you don't, sweetie. I don't like it either."

"Neither do I," replied a voice from the hallway as everyone turned to see Jillian enter the room. Curtis' first instinct was to throw himself at her feet and beg for mercy. Instead, he managed a contrite, "Jillian, I've missed you so much!" The two high school sweethearts hugged each other in the usual way and felt the usual twinges of comfort and joy, then stepped out into the hallway where they could talk.

Curtis returned to the Curtis of old as he quipped, "Let me look at you, my fair one! Yep! The same silly face, the same funny smile, the same pretty girl," he gushed.

"I'm sorry about your dad and grandma," a nonplussed Jillian replied.

"Oh, they're still here and will be for a long time. They're fighters! *Trust me!*"

After a pause as awkward as the comment that created it, Jillian pressed on, "So how have you been, Curtis? We haven't talked much since you… went away."

"Well, I've been busy with classes – you know how it is," answered Curtis, searching for understanding but not counting on it. "And how are *you* doing, my little chickadee?"

"I'm okay. Are you okay, Curtis? You seem a little jittery."

"It's just...coming home to *all of this*" as Curtis gestured at the surroundings, "I guess I'm not myself."

"So how long will you be staying?"

"Until grandma is home and dad is sitting at the head of the table again," Curtis answered with authority.

"Are we going to get through this, Curtis?" Jillian asked.

"Sure we are. We have a good rescue plan!"

"I mean are *we* going to get through this, Curtis?"

"Why wouldn't we, my queen?"

"I don't know," Jillian replied, looking into his eyes, searching for the truth. "You tell me."

CHAPTER 20

THE LOCAL 5-O'CLOCK NEWS FOCUSED on the shooting and chase at the Mexican border. The TV reporter explained what little they knew: "Two of McCall's militiamen, who were patrolling the border in their Humvee, had stopped a van carrying drugs. They were fired upon by the van, returned fire and chased it to the edge of the Rio Grande, where the occupants attempted to cross the river in a motorized dingy. One of the drug runners was killed and the other was pursued by Capt. Jeb Moultrie who jumped into the dingy as it left the shore.

There is no further word on the fate of the Captain or of the pursued individual. The Republic of Texas is working through diplomatic channels with the government of Mexico to ascertain the whereabouts of Capt. Moultrie. Security at the border has been increased. At the moment we have the proverbial "Mexican Standoff."

Pres. McCall has issued a statement saying, quote:

> "We demand an immediate response from the government of Mexico regarding the disappearance of Capt. Jeb Moultrie. Any delay in this matter will result in decisive action being taken by the Republic of Texas. Capt. Moultrie was simply doing his duty defending our border when his vehicle was attacked by drug runners

who illegally crossed over the border from Mexico. His pursuit of them took him into the Rio Grande, and he has not been heard from since. This was not an attack on the country of Mexico but rather a defense of ours. If you have detained our officer or are holding him as a hostage, we will come and get him. I recommend you follow the advice lettered on the side of Capt. Moultrie's command vehicle…"Don't Mess with Texas!"

The president of Mexico is unlike the president of most countries. He doesn't know what is going on across large parts of his nation at any given time. Much of it is out of his control. What he does know is there are violent drug lords warring with each other across all of Mexico. He knows their criminal ways have instilled fear in a land that has become the ongoing host of a drug-running marathon that reaches from the jungles of Colombia to the streets of Central America to the finish line at the Rio Grande Valley in the Republic of Texas. The Mexican border patrol and police are simply unable to keep up with the swift, cunning, violent drug cartels and their soldiers that are running rampant across Mexico today.

That's where the Campesinos come in. These vigilante groups are made up of local farmers and angry victims who have had enough of the lawlessness they are forced to live with and decided to take the law into their own hands. Their primary objective is to seek out and destroy as many drug dealers, runners and their soldiers as possible. Campesinos are not endorsed by the official Mexican authorities but they are supported by many of the "locals" across the country, who see the masked Campesino as a legendary figure who has come to their rescue. This is the group that took Jeb Moultrie into custody on the Mexican side of the Rio Grande.

As much as vigilante groups might be welcomed by their countrymen, they are still a bunch of dangerous individuals. Many take delight in the sheer violence of it all, and some have been known to shoot tourists for failing to stop at roadside checkpoints. Any vigilante group will include "enforcers" who instill fear in anyone unfortunate enough to cross their path. This element of this particular band of Campesinos saw Jeb and his drug-laden dingy as evidence of a bought-and-paid-for cartel connection.

They blindfolded him and took him to a vacant building in a lawless part of town for questioning.

"Who are you?" one stout, intense Campesino demanded to know. "My name is Jeb Moultrie of Sugarfield, Texas. I am a Captain in McCall's Militia," Jeb answered, pointing to his military fatigues.

"You lie! The uniform means nothing. Anyone can buy it. Did someone buy you? Who? Where you get these drugs?" the questioner insisted.

"My name is Jeb Moultrie of Sugarfield, Texas. I am a Captain in McCall's Militia," Jeb repeated.

The questioner grabbed hold of Jeb, threw him into a holding cell and locked the door. "You will answer to Cabecilla," he threatened.

As Jeb lay there on the concrete floor a million thoughts ran through his head: "Why did I chase the guy into the river? He gets away and I'm left holding the bag. How do I signal the militia? I don't even know where I am. How do I get out of here? Who the hell is Cabecilla? And last but not least, where are Batman and Robin when you need them?"

While JJ and the militia were formulating plans for military intervention in search of their captain, Curtis had an idea of his own. He went next door to see Frank and told him his plan. "Good Neighbor Frank" was totally in favor of trying to get Jeb Moultrie out of the tough spot he was in, if at all possible, and of avoiding any and all hostilities at the border. Curtis' plan was simple enough, though the chances of success seemed low.

"So," Frank replied, after listening to the skullduggery. "The two of us just walk right in the front door. We cross the border and start snooping around."

"Essentially, yes" replied Curtis. "There are a lot of poor people right across the border who might have seen something - or heard something - and would gladly sell their information. A few pesos go a long way down there," explained Curtis.

"It all sounds a little lame, Curtis."

"Hey, I admit I'm not James Bond, and we don't have an Aston Martin. Another air rescue isn't possible either; we don't even know where he is. So we'll go in and take a look around. What have we got to lose, other than our passports, our freedom and a week-end of running errands and mowing the lawn?"

"Well, when you put it that way......" Frank replied with a shrug and a grin, "Let's roll!" Batman and Robin, together again, bumped fists, shook hands and exchanged high-fives as they split up to tell their families about their newest action adventure.

Frank gave Emma a rough outline of their plan, and while she wasn't crazy about the idea, Frank assured her they were just looking for information and they would be back home in a day, one way or the other. Curtis told his family the same thing and got the same reaction. The horn blew at mid-day as Frank picked up Curtis in his SUV and headed for Mexico. Four hours later they reached McAllen, Texas and got in line to cross the border into Mexico.

When they got up to the gate, Curtis explained the purpose of their visit was tourism. They would see some sights, visit some restaurants and return before the weekend was over. The border guard looked at Frank, examined his ID and clarified "Frank Kaz - marcz?"

"Yes, Kazmarczyk," answered Frank.

"And you are Curtis Moultrie?"

"Yes," answered Curtis.

The guard looked at Curtis' papers more closely. "From Sugarfield, Texas?"

"Yes," Curtis replied again, feeling a bit uneasy.

The border guard motioned for them to wait, picked up the phone and said something in Spanish. Curtis and Frank eyed each other, apprehensively. The guard hung up the phone and said, "You will go with these men".

Curtis and Frank looked at the two men with rifles and crisscrossed ammunition belts who had come out from the booth, and correctly concluded that this was not the kind of help they were hoping for.

"Your vehicle will be impounded," the border guard told them as the armed men motioned for Frank and Curtis to exit the vehicle, which they did in stunned silence. As Frank's SUV was moved off to the side, he and Curtis were shepherded into a truck with searchlights on the roof and driven from the gate onto a side road.

"What's going on?" Curtis asked. "Where are you taking us?"

"We are just tourists," Frank insisted. "Just here for the weekend."

Their silent captors stared straight ahead as they sped away from the border and headed for Reynosa, a town that in spite of its welcoming Church's Chicken, Home Depot and Walmart stores, is entirely under control of the drug cartels.

Every week, running gun battles erupt in this city of 600,000 people between the Los Metros and Los Rojos gangs, both vying for prominence with the drug lords of the Gulf Cartel. SUVs loaded with gunmen roam the streets and attack each other at will. Residents remain indoors. They plug into social media to keep up to date with the most violent areas referred to as SDR or "situations of risk". A smart phone app called "Zello" enables citizens to operate their cell phones like walkie-talkies and ask about security conditions around the city. After gunfights, bodies are routinely thrown into vehicles and driven away.

Frank and Curtis felt as though they were traveling through a war zone - which they were - as they observed men in hoodies with cell phones in one hand and automatic rifles in the other directing citizens to take cover. As their Campesino paddy wagon roared out of town, a convoy of vehicles filled with gunmen was headed in the opposite direction, leaving rapid machine gun fire and bomb blasts in its wake. The police were nowhere to be seen. To deal with this kind of mayhem, the army would have to be sent in, and even then the outcome couldn't be assured. Frank and Curtis were stunned by what they were witnessing as they tried to imagine what might be waiting for them down the road.

They didn't have to wait long to find out, as the pickup truck came to a skidding halt in front of a dilapidated building on the outskirts of town. Frank and Curtis were rushed into a small, windowless room, dingy and bare except for a single metal desk, worn-out file cabinet and two broken down wooden chairs into which Frank and Curtis were forcibly seated. One of the armed captors remained in the room while the other went down the hallway toward the back of the building. He entered a second room which contained a prison cell and three other Campesinos, who were in on Jeb's capture the day before and were now standing guard over every breath he took.

The Cabecilla emerged from a room across from the prisoner's. He was the leader of this particular band of Campesinos, which like all vigilante groups was a ragtag collection of men who wanted to fight but had no real training, discipline or leadership skills. When groups like this come across a person who has the intelligence, resolve and leadership qualities they lack, they intuitively anoint him Cabecilla and they follow his orders.

Another perceived strength of this particular leader was his knowledge of how the drug runners made their connections in the north, which he had observed during the years he had lived there. And so, all eyes were on him as he looked at the prisoner and the prisoner looked at him for the very first time. "Oh... my...God," Jeb Moultrie stammered.

The Cabecilla bent down and leaned in until he was within an inch of Jeb's face, then asked in somewhat broken English, "So, how...is...my Maria?"

While Jeb was struggling to assimilate the sight of Hector Estrada in his face, and wondering how he would answer the man he put on the bus to Mexico along with his wife months ago, Frank and Curtis were led into the same room.

Hector continued his questioning: "It is not good to be taken away... is it Capt. Moultrie?" then turned his attention to the two other prisoners in the room and approached them. To Curtis he said, "You are the son. You live next door to my Maria."

"Yes, I am. I do!" Curtis cautiously answered.

Then it was Frank's turn. "Hello, Mr. Kazmarczyk," Hector said, as he extended his hand. It is good to see you again. How is Mrs. Kazmarczyk? She is a wonderful teacher, a wonderful person."

"Yes, she is," answered Frank as he grasped Hector's hand. "She is well, thank you."

"Juanita and I thank you and your wife again for taking our Maria into your home. I know she is happy."

"She is doing very well, Mr. Estrada, "but she is looking forward to the day her parents return."

"Yes, we are, too. Now you see what we are always trying to escape from in Mexico. I told my men to drive through Reynosa, so you see. Now is time for you to go back, with Curtis - and his father," as Hector cast a meaningful glance at Jeb. "I will explain to my men that we have no fight with you."

Jeb hugged his son, shook hands with Frank and nodded to Hector. The ride back to the border, in a more circuitous route, was uneventful. And the ride home in Frank's SUV was quiet and contemplative, as they all had come to a new understanding of the violence they were sending people back into, or were keeping them from escaping...a world much wilder than the Wild West ever was.

CHAPTER 21

CAPT. JEB MOULTRIE'S HOMECOMING WAS prime-time news on television and in the newspapers.

* **Captain Courageous Dumps Drug Runner into Rio Grande!**
* **Moultrie Runs Down Cartel in Wave-Runner Humvee!**
* **Militia Man turns Frogman in Drug Bust!**
* **Jeb Moultrie says NO to Drugs!**

Jeb Moultrie's exploits were well-chronicled by Zeke Hogan. Speaking to a cadre of reporters in front of the Moultrie home, he described Jeb's heroics as *Fantastic, Mind-boggling* and *Unafraid.* "He drove that Humvee into the Rio Grande like it was nothin' but hot asphalt. We're half-driving, half-floating and the water's splashin' like some kind of roller coaster ride. I proceed to shoot one of the banditos and the next thing I know the Captain leaps out of the Humvee and lands on their scrawny little boat like the *Great White* from "Jaws."

He's poundin' the guy, and takin' a few in return, and before I know it they disappear in the dark. I wait. I watch. I see nothin'. I hear nothin'.

That's when I contact the other units on patrol and we start formulating a rescue plan. Right, JJ?"

The array of news microphones suddenly angled sharply to the left as precisely as a rank of wooden soldiers on parade, as JJ Moultrie stepped forward. "Although things turned out for the best - thanks to my little brother and Frank," JJ answered, as he nodded to the two-man rescue party standing behind him - "we were planning on going into Mexico and getting him out of there by whatever means necessary."

"What means might those have been?" asked a reporter.

"That's classified information," replied JJ. "I can't give you an answer about any military action we *might* have taken...other than to say we would have confronted the responsible parties and taken them out," JJ clarified.

"When you say *taken them out* does that include *blowing them up*, if you thought it was necessary?" asked a woman reporter.

JJ paused for a moment, looked at the reporter who had asked the question and replied, "I didn't say anything about blowing anybody up," Miss??"

"Bailey," the reporter replied. "Kay Bailey. But would you? Have you *ever* blown anybody up Mr. Moultrie?"

JJ continued staring at the reporter from KXOTV and said, "I think it's time to turn the interview over to my brother, Curtis. He's the real hero. Along with Frank. And my dad, of course. Let's hear from them."

Curtis proceeded to relate his and Frank's story of capture, confrontation and resolution. "Basically, they let us go. They knew our dad wasn't part of any drug ring."

"So, it was a case of mistaken identity?" another reporter asked.

"You could say that. Right, dad?"

Jeb looked around at the reporters, his family and his neighbors and said, "Right. I chased a drug runner. He got away. They saw me alone on the boat with the drugs and thought I was involved. Yeah. Mistaken identity." Jeb ended the interview with a short summation of his experience: "Going after bad guys is the right thing to do; it's important to stand up for your God and country; if I had to do it all over again - I would. Only next time, I'd probably be a little bit more cautious."

As the crowd on the lawn scattered and departed, JJ approached Kay

Bailey and said, "When are you going to leave us alone?" to which Kay Bailey replied, "When you admit what you did."

JJ turned, walked up the front stairs and joined the rest of the Moultries in the dining room for a feast fit for a king, if not for a Captain. Jenny said "grace," and they all thanked their lucky stars for the pluck of Jeb Moultrie, the luck of Curtis and Frank and the Duck & Oyster Gumbo that was in the oven.

Dinnertime was upbeat, but somewhat anxious. Everyone was still concerned about grandma Taylor who had just been released from the hospital and was stoically sitting in her wheelchair in the dining room. Her spirits brightened considerably when Jeb walked into the room. He immediately went over and told her he was perfectly fine and that she needn't worry about him anymore. Her Number One Job was to get well!

"I'll do my best, Jeb. It's so wonderful to see you!" grandma acknowledged as Jeb guided her wheelchair to her place at the table.

"And you keep looking after her, grandpa Taylor."

"Yes, sir. Right away, sir!" grandpa Taylor replied, snapping off a smart salute.

Jenny was happy to see the entire family together again - including the boys' girlfriends - as she said a silent prayer of thanks.

Jeb stood up from the table and proposed a toast to his loving, understanding wife; dutiful son, JJ; Superhero rescue team; loving grandparents; and beauty queens Jillian, Rita, Emma and Camilla and her friend, Maria. "*Cheers!*"

The repast included crabmeat salad, fried green tomatoes, southern pan-fried potatoes, and the aforementioned specialty of the house: duck and oyster gumbo. JJ and Curtis had their eyes on the banana split pie from the get-go, but were waved off by their eagle-eyed mom until the time was right. The girls opted for bread pudding, and everyone else tried a little bit of both, with some saving room for the pecan pralines.

The dinner conversation revolved around the daring deeds of the father of the house. "I've been telling you for years to learn how to swim," remarked Jenny.

Number One Son boasted, "If I was riding shotgun they never would've reached the boat"....and Frank, of Superhero fame exclaimed, "Holy vigilantes, Batman! They got the drop on us!"

Even though everyone knew how Jeb's exploits ended, everyone still loved to hear the story told over and over again.

After the table was cleared and the dishes were done, everyone adjourned to their respective corners. Jeb and Jenny gave her mom and dad some additional moral support. "You can count on us for whatever you need," Jeb assured his in-laws. "We know you're facing some big hospital bills. We can help!"

"Jenny, the hospital bill alone is $35,000," grandma Taylor revealed. "There's no Medicare anymore. We have to pay!"

"It'll be all right," assured Jenny. "There's always a way."

Curtis and Jillian found a quiet spot out back to catch up on their news of the day. "Are things ever going to get back to normal, Curtis?" inquired Jillian.

"They are already, sweetie pie," answered an unconcerned Curtis. "Sure, there were a couple of bumps in the road, but dad and grandma are back on track now."

"It seems that *your* track is still heading in a different direction than mine," clarified Jillian.

"Not really. We're living in two different worlds right now, but that's only temporary. I've got some new life experiences; you've got some new life experiences."

"What kind of new life experiences have you had, Curtis?" Jillian wanted to know.

"Well, there is this journalism club that I'm part of. We want to write stories…exposes …about what's going on in the country. Amber says we can make a big difference in the world. We have to get to the bottom of things, uncover the truth and tell it the way it is. We're very passionate."

"Are you?" quizzed Jillian.

"Yes…this immigration mess we just went through is a perfect example. Amber thinks I can help get information about what is going on. I do, too."

"Really? Is that what Amber thinks?" prodded Jillian.

"Absolutely! She tells me that all the time."

"So you spend a lot of time with Amber?" asking a rhetorical question.

"Sure, I mean we meet at least a couple of times a week. I mean, we *all* meet," Curtis quickly clarified. "There are other people in the group, too. There's DayQuan, he's a real good friend of Amber's. He's gay."

"Oh, so he's a good friend, but he's gay," Jillian corroborated.

"Yeah," Curtis hurried on, "then there is Omar from Pakistan, Indira from Calcutta, Soon-Lee from China, Vince, Wayne, Al, Ken, Joan. It's a big group. Huge group! But Amber's the leader"

"Is she?"

"Oh yeah, she's very smart…you'd like her!"

"Would I, Curtis?" Jillian probed with an inquisitive stare.

"Sure, you'll see. I've got a plan, but…here I am babbling on and on about me and not asking about what you're doing. So, what's it like for *you* at South Texas State?"

"It's very good, Curtis. I'm always busy with interesting classes and fun people. Lots of fun people. There are a couple of cool football players in the fraternity next door."

"Fraternity? You go to fraternities?"

"I do." "I thought you had to be in a sorority in order to do that," Curtis asked, posing a rhetorical question of his own.

"I am. I'm pledging Delta Omega."

"You're pledging? A sorority?" asked a startled Curtis.

"Yep! I'm going to a social mixer on Saturday before the football game. We're playing Oklahoma Southern."

"Really? Saturday? I thought we could go out Saturday before I head north."

"I've got plans, Curtis, just like you've got plans."

"So, how about we go to the game together?"

"You mean…a date? Are you asking me out on a date?"

"Okay. Sure. I am. Yes."

Jillian paused for effect, then replied, "Alright. You can pick me up at Theta Chi."

"Theta Chi," Curtis repeated. "Sounds fancy."

"Yes, it is. I can introduce you to Jason, their pledge chairman. We were going to go to the game together, but I can cancel. *You'd like him,*" Jillian assured, twisting the dagger.

"Would I?" Curtis responded weakly, wondering if this was the way it was going to be from now on between the inseparable high school couple who signed each other's yearbooks, "Love Always."

Meanwhile, Frank and Emma had made themselves comfortable in two white wicker chairs on the front porch and were sharing a small dish of the remaining pecan pralines. The sun was on its magnificent downward trajectory when a bustling little chatterbox cozied up to them.

"Mrs. Kazmarczyk…Maria told me she likes living at your house," Camilla confided.

"That's nice to hear, Camilla. We hope her mom and dad get to move back soon. That's where she really belongs," Emma replied.

"When are they coming?" wondered Camilla.

"It's going to take some time," Frank explained.

"How much time?" Camilla insisted.

"Well, first Mr. and Mrs. Estrada have to apply for a visa. They have to go through some special courts for that and they may have to hire a lawyer, which costs money. Then they have to prove they can speak English."

"They can!" volunteered Camilla. "Maria was teaching them!"

Frank continued, "I know. Mr. Estrada's English is pretty good. I don't know about Mrs. Estrada though…and then they have to prove they have a job."

"How do they do that?" asked Camilla.

"Someone will have to speak up for them."

"Like you spoke up for Maria?"

"Yes, it won't be easy. They were here illegally in the first place, so they will have to wait. It may take…years!"

"Years?" asked an unbelieving Camilla. "Will you keep Maria that long?"

"If we have to, yes," answered Emma.

"Good. Maria is teaching me science! I like it. Maria showed me her science book. It has some good stories in it. I like stories!"

Jenny Moultrie, who had wandered over, heard just enough of the conversation to try to divert it. "Stories are just stories, Camilla. They are make-believe. Like your "Cat got your Tongue?" book. They aren't real," advised Jenny.

"How do you know, mom? Maybe the cat is real. Maybe the little hand that's millions of years old in Maria's science book is real!"

"Camilla, we can talk about this some other day," Jenny suggested.

"Yes, we can," Emma agreed, "any time you want," looking first at Camilla then over at Jenny.

As quick as a cat in a hat, the conversation abruptly turned to the old standbys: the weather ("it's been so nice, hasn't it, mid-80s, possible showers"); the price of groceries ("do you believe $8 a gallon for milk, who can pay these prices!"); and the upcoming South Texas State vs. Oklahoma Southern football game ("Jillian is going...with Curtis! They make such a nice couple. They belong together.")

Another person who had no interest in discussing the laws of immigration or of science at this particular time was Maria. She was sitting in a corner of the living room with grandma Taylor, reading to her from the book she brought from home. *"The Lord himself goes before you and will be with you; He will never leave you nor forsake you. Do not be afraid; do not be discouraged. Deuteronomy 31:8."* Grandma Taylor was lost in reverie, listening intently to the words Maria was speaking, amazed at her thoughtfulness and overwhelmed by her faith. *"May the God of hope fill you with all joy and peace as you trust in Him, so that you may overflow with hope by the power of the Holy Spirit. Romans 15:13.* As Marie closed her Bible, grandma Taylor put her hand on Maria's hand and smiled down upon her countenance through a veil of forgiveness and tears.

The final emotional connection of the day was the announcement by JJ Moultrie that he had asked Rita to marry him and that she had said..."*Yes!*" Any passersby would have thought someone in the Moultrie home had just won the lottery. When the whooping, hollering, crying and backslapping subsided, Rita capped off the best day anyone in the Moultrie family could ever remember with one final proclamation: "The wedding will be in two weeks!" And the pandemonium began all over again.

CHAPTER 22

CURTIS GOT UP EARLY SATURDAY morning, packed his bag for the
return trip to Kilmer, and sat down for a quick family breakfast. Between
bites of his Tex-Mex omelet and thick-sliced bacon, Curtis asked his mom
to please keep mailing the pecan pies and his grandparents to keep their
spirits up. Before he headed out the door, he briefly explained to his dad
what his journalism group was trying to do, and asked the question he'd
wanted to ask since the day he and Amber practically buried themselves
in the sand on Lake Michigan.

"I see, Curtis," his dad acknowledged. "And this will help you get
information for your story? I think I can help. I'll let you know."

"Thanks a million, dad!" Curtis gratefully replied. "Amber and the
group will be very happy."

"Who's Amber?" Curtis' dad felt obliged to ask.

"Oh, just a journalism friend. You'd like her!"

"Would I?" Jeb asked in a tone that instinctively turned wary.

"See you in two weeks," Curtis advised, referring to JJ's wedding.

"Oh. Right! The big day! Don't forget to order your tux. The Best Man
can't show up in boots and blue jeans!" reminded Jeb.

"Well, not blue jeans anyway," Curtis shot back as he jumped into
his dad's SUV. "I'll bring the car back tomorrow. JJ is taking me to the
airport!"

Jeb nodded and waved, "Say Hello to Jillian. You be good to that girl!"

"Got it!" Curtis replied for the last time, as he hit the road for the drama that accompanies two of the greatest rivalries anywhere: South Texas State vs. Oklahoma Southern; and man vs. woman.

Every other car on the road displayed a South Texas State flag flapping in the breeze, or a bumper decal or hand-scrawled rear window battle cry. The prevailing sentiment seemed to be: *you're not doing fine, Oklahoma. Oklahoma, not OK!*

But these were just the preliminaries. The STS campus itself was alive with orange and black-colored shirts, socks, sweats, stickers, bodies, faces, hair. It was like aliens from the planet Orange had had taken over every life form, conveyance and body covering. As difficult as it was to stand out in this crowd, Curtis did so as he walked into the Theta Chi pre-kickoff party looking for Jillian - in his purple and silver Kilmer Tee.

Jillian, in her own orangeade-colored Delta Omega shirt, was happy to see him."You're not at the wrong game are you, Curtis? We're not playing Kilmer," chided the new sorority pledge.

"No. I'm in the right place - because you're here," replied Curtis.

"Well aren't you the sweetest thing? You northern boys certainly know how to charm a lady," Jillian observed in her best Scarlet O'Hara delivery.

"You must be one of those Southern Belles I've heard so much about," replied Curtis, following her lead. "You are a real beauty! Aren't you supposed to be wearing a big hoop skirt and twirling a parasol?"

"I do declare, you are a very forward young man aren't you, Mr. Moultrie?" Jillian segued from southern belle to smarty pants, as she reached for the arm of a person passing by and said, "Allow me to introduce you to a true southern gentleman. This is Bradley Moore, pledge chairman of Theta Chi. Mr. Moore, I'd like you to meet Mr. Curtis Moultrie."

"Hello Curtis," Brad responded, as he extended his hand and glanced at Curtis' shirt. "Welcome to Texas."

"Hello, Bradley. Nice to meet you. But I *am* from Texas. Sugarfield! I go to school at Kilmer College," explained Curtis.

"Why?" Brad asked, with some interest.

"It's a long story," Curtis answered.

"And getting longer by the minute," Jillian added.

"So you're rooting for our Bulldogs?" asked Bradley.

"Absolutely," Curtis replied, "Oklahoma Southern is going down!" "No contest!"

Bradley seconded the motion. "Nice meeting you, Curtis."

"You, too." responded Curtis.

"See you, Jillian," promised Brad. "Bye, Brad," promised Jillian.

"He seems like a nice guy," Curtis offered.

"I told you that you'd like him," Jillian reminded him.

"Touché," Curtis acquiesced, "shall we move on?"

"Let's," Jillian agreed, "we've got a football game to win. Or, as we like to say around here, *Sic 'em Bulldogs!*"

"Or, as we like to say at Kilmer, *Repel them, repel them, make them relinquish the ball!*"

"You don't really say that, do you?"

"I don't! Some do. Not me. Nope," grinned Curtis.

"I hope not," laughed Jillian, for the first time in a long time.

As they continued on their way to the stadium, they passed the parking area which was jammed with tailgating parties. Again, the orange and black on banners and large tents, coolers, kegs, and open grills full of steak, chicken, hot dogs, burgers, peppers, onions, the works. That is, about 75% of them were South Texas State tents. There were also similar cooking setups featuring the red and gray colors of Oklahoma Southern. Everybody was wearing their school colors, and everybody was tossing footballs around. Inevitably, one pass from an Oklahoma Southern quarterback "wanna-be" was thrown over the head of his intended receiver and took out a South Texas cooler before connecting with a T-bone steak on an open grill and sending it into the dirt like a middle linebacker dropping a scat back.

When the Oklahoma Southern QB asked for "A little help!" in returning the football, he just fanned the flames of ruined-T-bone discontent. Instead of tossing the football back with a soft lob, the Texas grill-master fired a nice tight spiral right into the Southern fan's grill, scattering his meat and potatoes and catching him in the face.

The offended OSU QB took a bead on the Texan and let fly with another football that broke one of the his tent poles, which brought the house down on a bunch of unhappy Bulldogs, who returned fire, and just that quick, footballs and epithets were flying everywhere. And then it got personal.

"No wonder you Texas assholes seceded, you can't even shoot straight," observed one fiery Oklahoma Southern fanatic.

"We're not the ones killing babies in clinics, you God-forsaken murderers!" responded a South Texas backer who took down the Oklahoma QB with a flying tackle.

"Yeah, and you're blowing up our clinics like the cowards you are!" was another rejoinder heard above the yelling and cussing and punching and tackling that spread like wildfire to other tents as the action intensified and the hits were meted out as viciously as any of the players might deliver in the stadium.

Two of the few observers who stayed out of the fray turned their attention from the melee toward each other as Curtis cogently remarked to Jillian, "And we thought we had problems!"

CHAPTER 23

WHEN TEXAS RE-INVENTED ITSELF THREE years earlier, its citizens had a lot of confidence in their future. At that time, the state of Texas was the leading oil producer in the nation and its refineries processed a good portion of the country's gasoline. The state of Texas was also a leading producer of computer chips and communications products and a leading supplier of beef, poultry, hogs, grains, fruit, paper and plastics. The space industry was still vibrant.

People felt they would have enough of what they needed to be self-sufficient. But the price for this self-sufficiency was high, as some major corporations in the Republic of Texas decided to relocate their offices. Ironically, the more labor-intensive companies remained. In a reversal of fortune, it become cheaper to make certain production-line products in the Republic of Texas because its new Lone Star Dollar was worth less than a United States Dollar. The exchange ratio had stabilized at around 3 to 1: it took three Lone Star Dollars to equal the buying power of one US Dollar (as Curtis found out to his dismay when he first offered to buy his new friends in Evanston a pizza and they jokingly told him, "Your money is no good here!")

After complaining for years about US corporations sending jobs overseas for the cheap labor, the same scenario was now being played out in the newly minted Republic of Texas. Only now the cheap workforce was as close as the border. And more than ever before, they wanted in.

Then there was the issue of rising costs. Without federal funding, the cost of providing public schools, colleges, highways, postal services and hospitals fell entirely on the tax payers of the new Republic. Nothing took a bigger hit than health care. Without employers providing health care benefits and the new government not providing Medicare or Medicaid benefits, everyone was entirely on their own. This led to tough times for many people.

For instance, before Texas left the union, it had the largest number of uninsured residents in the United States: 27%. In three years, that number had doubled. Those who could not afford to buy a private health insurance plan had two choices: don't get sick; or if you do, move in with your family as former presidential candidate Mitt Romney had suggested, and as grandma and grandpa Taylor actually did.

The Taylors had just spent a large part of their savings on doctor and hospital bills for grandma Taylor's heart attack. Her health was now being monitored on a more regular basis, adding additional financial strain to their dwindling pocketbook. Grandpa was also taking new meds for his failing health, and his onset Alzheimer's meant it wouldn't be long before the Taylors could simply not take care of themselves physically or financially. Moving in with Jeb and Jenny was the only option.

They took Curtis' room and joined in all of the Moultrie's games and activities, which brought the family even closer together. The next big decision revolved around who would look after grandma and gramps during the daytime. Jeb went to his office every morning even though he had little to do. As major corporations in the Houston area downsized, so did Jeb's business. There simply wasn't any new building going on. Jeb tried to fall back on remodeling, which was how he got started in the first place, but there wasn't much happening there, either. The building blocks of the Republic of Texas were "On Hold" pending further developments.

With Jeb's income taking a hit, Jenny decided to look for a job. The day care center she used to work for had also gotten smaller and was getting by with less staff. After sending out numerous resumes, Jenny was lucky enough to find a part-time job with a home healthcare company. They provided home health "companions" to people who had health issues but couldn't afford to move into an assisted living facility. The company Jenny now worked for sent their companions to people's homes to watch over them on an hourly basis. Jenny scheduled the appointments and kept track of all the paperwork. Ironically, this was the kind of attention her mother and father needed and why Jenny could only work part-time. She already had that full-time job at home.

As time went by, belts were tightened and expectations were lowered for a lifestyle that seemed attainable just a few short years ago. On the other side of the coin, the time everyone now spent together in the Moultrie home was *quality* time.

The Taylors felt closer to their granddaughter than ever before. Jeb helped grandpa Taylor keep his mind active by constantly asking questions about how he had met his wife, his experiences as a father to Jenny, and his opinion on who was going to make it to the Super Bowl. Gramps was still alert in some areas, and he always perked up when answering questions and providing details about his best friend and lifelong sweetheart, Betty Jo.

Jenny helped her melancholy mother feel loved and relevant by asking for her cooking tips and special recipes and for her child-rearing advice regarding the ever-popular, fun- seeking Camilla.

Late in the evening Jeb and Jenny would reconnect and sit at the kitchen table to go over their finances, as most people do who have bills to pay, grandparents to house and care for, a young child to raise and a wedding rehearsal dinner to pay for. In other words …life.

CHAPTER 24

BRIDE-TO-BE RITA MCCLAIN AWOKE TO the sounds of twittering mockingbirds - and friends - on the biggest day of her life. "RU up?… did JJ call in sick? lol…can't wait to see the dress…your bff.…"

Rita always was a popular girl. Her fresh-faced beauty and outgoing personality attracted admirers from both sides of the sexual divide. She was a pretty, petite dark-eyed sparkler who liked outdoor activities and sports and could catch a trout or a softball with equal aplomb. She had many suitors. After dozens of dances, splash parties, movies and dinner dates with different young men, Rita found happiness right in her own backyard with her Sugarfield school mate/soul mate, JJ Moultrie.

He was passionate about many things, especially Rita. They had that spark. They loved each other, and they understood each other so well, that even through the Dark Days of the abortion fight and flight they never questioned each other's motives or methods. It was the sort of thing that, unless you had gone through it yourself, you couldn't appreciate how deep the feelings about "pro life" and "pro choice" can be. If anything, Rita and JJ's feelings for each other were strengthened by the experience.

Rita now knew that JJ absolutely would go to the ends of the earth for her. And JJ knew that Rita would listen to him, come with him and live with him with open lines of communication - and no regrets. A formula for a successful marriage, if there ever was one.

Rita's parents had come to feel the same way about JJ. They had always admired his devotion to their daughter. The extremes he went to in his pursuit of her salvation (notwithstanding the horrible aftermath which no one believed he was responsible for) gave Rita the focus and inner strength to do the right thing, as far as he and her parents were concerned. That was what sealed the deal for them.

The Moultries had always liked Rita's politeness and pleasant manner. And they never forgot how excited their nervous young son became when Rita said she would go to the Junior Prom with him. Who would have imagined that a few years later, instead of pinning a corsage on her dress, JJ would be placing a diamond ring on her finger.

Rita started getting ready for the 2 o'clock church ceremony right after breakfast. She took her time putting on her makeup. She double-checked, then triple-checked her nails. Her mother brushed her soft, silky raven hair until it was perfect in every way. And then she started all over again, all the while reminiscing about her own special day a generation ago. "You look positively radiant, my dear. I know exactly how you feel and how beautiful it is all going to be," she promised.

Camilla was mimicking every move Rita made. She was doing her own primping and admiring herself in front of the full-length mirror. The flower girl had to be perfect, too! She took her bridesmaid's dress off the hanger and held it up to herself. It was a wonderfully soft, long chiffon dress with a beaded neckline. The color was Wisteria, and it brightened her face with sunshine as she held it up under her chin.

"You look beautiful, honey," Rita said. "Like a flower," added her mother. "You will be the apple of Jamie Rawlin's eye."

Camilla scrunched up her nose at the thought of walking down the aisle with the 5-year old ring bearer. "He's just a baby," replied Camilla. "I'm going into second grade!"

The other four bridesmaids kept poking their heads into Rita's room to check on her progress and to model their own strapless, diaphanous gowns like blossoms on a wisteria-covered wedding arch.

While the ladies were buzzing around the Queen Bee, the men at the Moultrie house had some details of their own to attend to. Some were still recovering from the previous evening's wedding rehearsal dinner, a celebration that went off without a hitch - unless you consider JJ and his supporting cast stopping off at a bar across the street for a lengthy pre-party toast - a hitch.

Jeb Moultrie had spared no expense, and nearly went into debt doing it. He rented a large party room in Rita's favorite restaurant, replete with fried chicken, barbecue ribs, sliced beef, cornucopias of fruit and salads, kegs of beer and carafes of wine which kept the party going long after closing time, led by Zeke, one of JJ's stoutest militia man drinking buddies.

JJ's "Best Man," Curtis, made sure he was not over-served and got home at a reasonable hour. Everyone thanked everyone for the invitation. Jeb and Jenny toasted JJ and Rita, who toasted her parents, who toasted the bridal party, who toasted the guests, who toasted the man in the moon, and a good time was had by all.

Now...here...today, everyone was on the clock. The father of the groom had the makings of a great tuxedo all laid out on his bed. He put on the pants, shirt, vest, studs, and the rest, the way he thought they went on, and when there were no extra pieces still lying on the bed he knew it was mission accomplished. JJ needed some help cinching up the cummerbund and adjusting the thankfully pre-tied bow tie. Curtis was good. He had already made his own wardrobe adjustments. Four times.

They drove to the church together and met the rest of JJ's stand-up guys there. When they walked into the narthex they looked like a scene out of the latest penguin movie, as they strutted around with straight backs, tucked-in chins and startled looks as they tried to tell one from the other.

JJ wore a cream-colored vest and white tie versus the pure white and black everyone else had on. They all wore wisteria cummerbunds, which matched their bridal-party partners' dresses as they all paired off, waiting for their cue.

The church was filled to capacity as the organ unleashed its thunderous processional theme, and all celebrants craned their necks to see who would be the first to walk down the white linen-covered aisle.

It was Camilla, with her sweet smile, goldilocks hair and soft lavender dress, tossing wisteria blossoms into the air from a wicker basket on her arm. Her partner, Jamie, trudged along with one hand in his tiny tuxedo pocket, searching for a diamond ring.

The "ahhs" and "awws" said it all. Next came the grinning bridal party, arm-in-arm and as in-step as they could be, with JJ's friends paired up with Rita's friends on once-in-a-lifetime dates. Finally, the "Best Man" and "Maid of Honor" were sighted. Curtis looked dapper and proud and Susan, Rita's best friend, was beaming and obviously honored.

As the organ segued into "Here Comes the Bride," everyone stood and turned to see the most beautiful girl in the world. Rita was a vision in a snow white, lace-trimmed high-waist gown, beaded all over and fitted at the top and flared below the knees, giving her a "mermaid" look. The bride was as alluring and evocative as the dress she wore. Her soft smile and ephemeral presence tugged at every witness's heartstrings as she floated down the aisle on the arm of her strong, choked-up father.

From his vantage point, JJ felt frozen in time as the woman of his dreams slowly drifted toward him. They locked eyes, and the world around them disappeared, leaving only two kindred spirits moving closer together until they commingled into one, as the pastor would soon officially proclaim.

Their vows were exchanged reverently and expeditiously. Their thoughts were communicated telepathically, and by the time the pastor said "You may now kiss the bride," JJ imagined he already had.

The upbeat organ recessional sent JJ and Rita down the aisle and into a world of well-wishers, hand-shakers, kiss-planters, and party goers who turned the ensuing wedding reception into a rip-roaring, hootenanny that would have made Hank Williams, Sr. stand up and say "Howdy." Between the line dancing, square dancing and slow dancing, everybody did their part to blow the roof off the joint.

Two of the more enthusiastic celebrants called time out and went outside to the patio for a breath of fresh air. "Is this a great time or what?" Curtis asked his dance partner.

"I love it," answered Jillian. "They look perfect together."

"And who helped them get together, if you don't mind my asking?" asked Curtis.

"I give up. Who?" teased Jillian.

"Why, yours truly, of course! Remember my derring-do with ol' Frank?"

"I remember Frank flying JJ out of the frying pan," recalled Jillian.

"He certainly did," confirmed Curtis.

"And you went along for the ride," added Jillian.

"Well, I'd like to think I had a little more to do with it than that," insisted Curtis.

"Okay, I'll give you that much."

"So, don't I get a reward for my efforts?"

"What did you have in mind, Mr. Superhero?"

Curtis demonstrated what he had in mind by giving her a kiss that lasted longer than a pat of butter on a hot grill.

"Curtis, I didn't know you cared," declared a slightly ruffled Jillian.

"I didn't know you didn't know! Now *all these people* know," Curtis proudly explained, as he gestured toward the gathering, amused crowd.

"I think we should go back and face the music," Jillian decided with certitude.

"You mean…" Curtis started to reply, not certain of where she was headed.

"I mean *dance*, Curtis! Let's dance!"

"Yowsah, yowsah, ladies and gentlemen," Curtis theatrically proclaimed, "step right up and watch the finest dance team this side of the Rio Grande!" as they disappeared into the crowd.

On the other side of the patio the ravishing bride was thanking all the well-wishers for their thoughts and gifts. As she made her way through the diminishing crowd, a woman walked right up to her and said "Hello. Congratulations."

"I'm sorry," Rita said. I guess I don't know everyone here. Are you a friend of Curtis' or someone?"

"No. I'm a friend of yours," the woman replied.

"Of mine?" Rita questioned.

"Yes. I have some good advice for you. Clear up this business about JJ in Oklahoma. The FBI has put some undercover agents on the case."

"Who are you?" an astonished Rita replied. "Are you…that reporter?"

"Yes, I'm Kay Bailey from KXOTV. And I'm just trying to help."

"Why can't you people leave us alone!" Rita cried out. "This is our wedding day!"

"Then why ruin the rest of your life hiding out," Kay persisted.

"Look, Ms. Bailey, for the last time, JJ had nothing to do with the bombing of that clinic! Ask Jennifer Nelson."

Kay paused, then asked "Who is Jennifer Nelson?"

"She was there, too," answered Rita. "She has an Abortion Hotline website. I was talking with her just before I left with JJ."

"There is no record of a Jennifer Nelson being in the clinic," stated Kay. "Just the receptionist who was killed in the blast and another woman, who has recovered but can't remember anything."

"I'm telling you there was another person there," Rita insisted. "Jennifer Nelson was there! She knows JJ didn't do anything. She was the person who convinced me to go to that clinic. She set it all up. She knows me. She knows JJ. Find....her!!!!!"

"Alright, I'm sorry for interrupting your big day," Kay replied with some sincerity and some new questions forming in her mind. "I didn't know how else to reach you. Just think about what I'm telling you."

"And you think about what I am telling *you*," countered Rita.

"Alright, Rita. I'm sorry. Good night," Kay apologized, and left the reception with a totally different purpose than when she came in.

Rita and JJ's honeymoon was a compromise. Rita had always dreamed of going to Miami Beach, but due to circumstances beyond their control, i.e. - the FBI watching every U.S. airport and border - they settled on Jamaica.

The day after their wedding, JJ and Rita packed their swimsuits, flip flops and SPF50 and headed for George Bush Intercontinental Airport. They presented their Republic of Texas passports and received boarding passes for their non-stop flight to an island paradise. Four hours later they arrived at Sangster International Airport in Montego Bay. They took a cab to their all-inclusive resort and hit the beach like a couple of kids with visions of colorful tropical fish and unassailable sandcastles dancing in their heads.

Later that evening, a sunset dinner cruise on a catamaran left them in awe of God's glory as they viewed the remains of the day over Pina Coladas and superbly prepared fresh seafood, then came ashore to the soft sounds of steel drums and drifted off to dreamland in the arms of a wonderful world.

Day Two was as fresh and invigorating as Day One. After an outdoor breakfast of guava juice, poached eggs, thick-cut bacon and fresh pineapple, JJ and Rita signed up for adventure. A van picked them up at their hotel for a short ride to Dunn's River Falls, a series of waterfalls over and among rocks that people walk across, sometimes hand-in-hand with their guide, sometimes by their own fearless selves.

Every little waterfall is different. Some are light and showery. Some are more robust. You never know to what degree you will be drenched as you step from one rocky place to another. But the guides know. They slowly and purposely lead the ladies to one strategic position under one of the more powerful falls which suddenly pours down with enough force to literally knock the lady's swimsuit top completely off, to the shrieking surprise of the offended party - Rita! - and to the joy of any male observers - JJ and others! - who happened to be in the right place at the right time. The guides never cease to get a kick out of it themselves. Some say it even gets them bigger tips! The van ride back to the hotel was all abuzz over the primary attraction of Dunn's River Falls, which had made JJ and Rita some new friends, especially Rita, and especially male ones. Dinner invitations were extended to the honeymooners by two other couples, and the offer was accepted. They were to meet in the hotel lobby at 6 o'clock.

Until then, JJ and Rita decided to spend the rest of the day souvenir shopping, which turned out to be a little more depressing than they might have otherwise imagined. Souvenirs from most island nations are made by the natives themselves. This is also true in Jamaica, but here they all congregate around the hotels, and it can get a little uncomfortable making your way through the aggressive sellers. In a way, it reminded Rita of the poorer people just south of the Rio Grande, many of whom sell their beaded belts, bowls and carved figures on the streets of Mexico and in Texas. This, in turn, reminded Rita of another unfortunate incident - the recent run-in with Kay Bailey at the wedding. Rita had made up her mind not to bring up anything negative to JJ on their honeymoon, but everything changed that night - after dinner.

The three couples met as planned and agreed to have dinner in the hotel's open-air restaurant. The warm tropical breeze and setting sun did wonders for everyone's disposition. Everyone got better acquainted over Mai Tais and Red Stripe Beer. Suzie and Roger Wilkins from Atlanta got the ball rolling. "So, Rita," asked Roger grinning from ear to ear, "are you ready for a return engagement at Dunn's River Falls?"

Everyone chuckled at the memory as Rita shyly replied "When Hell freezes over I am. Why didn't you tell me what they were up to, JJ?"

"Hey, how was I supposed to know?" replied JJ. "The guide told me to get my camera ready, that's all."

"You knew!" Rita reacted, delivering JJ a solid elbow into his side.

After the group chuckling subsided, Suzie acknowledged that she and Roger, who said he was a bottling plant manager, were celebrating their 5th Wedding Anniversary, and that she wished nothing but the best for Rita and JJ on the road ahead. "Place your seat tray in its full and upright position, tighten your seat belt and prepare for a bumpy ride folks," advised Roger, and now it was his turn for a shot in the ribs, from Suzie.

Calvin and Caroline Mason were a few years older. Cal was "an attorney with a conscience" and Caroline ran a small gift shop in Washington, DC.

JJ gave the two couples a brief synopsis of his and Rita's backgrounds: met in high school; couldn't live without each other ("well, *I couldn't* anyway!"); owned a lawn service company; and lived in Sugarfield, Texas. That last part is what got everybody's attention.

"So, you're from the new Republic of Texas! From one southerner to another, do you miss being part of the great American south?" asked Roger.

"Not really," answered JJ. "We've always had a lot in common. Always will! Brothers-in-arms, and all that. But no, I don't regret going it alone. No offense, but Washington DC doesn't run our lives any more," as he shot a quick glance over at Calvin.

"None taken," answered Calvin. So how's life treating you down there?"

"Just fine," JJ replied. "We do as we please, and if we've got a problem, we fix it. Fast." "I see," responded Calvin.

"Speaking of problems, how are you handling the immigration situation down there? Wasn't that an issue you felt only you could resolve?"

"We're getting there, Calvin. Tightening up the borders, especially in the Rio Grande Valley."

"Isn't that where a Texas militia man crossed into Mexico and was captured?" inquired Calvin.

"He went after a drug dealer. That's all that happened!" JJ blurted out.

After a somewhat awkward pause, Caroline asked, "Wasn't an abortion clinic bombed recently...in Oklahoma? "Wasn't the suspect from Texas? Did they ever find him - or them?"

"No, there was never any proof of anything," assured JJ.

"Caroline and Calvin," Roger interjected in his slow and deliberate manner, "most southern folks put a lot of stock in their family values. Sometimes they get criticized for that and get blamed for things whether they did them or not. Isn't that about the size of it, JJ?"

"Yes, Roger" answered JJ, "you understand."

"Yes, I do," affirmed his former fellow countryman with a deep nod.

"Well then," the self-described attorney with a conscience quickly chimed in, "let us stop badgering the witness, and get to the meat of the matter, as in menus! Menus, please…" Calvin announced as he motioned for their waiter to come to the rescue.

The rest of the evening was spent in small talk about the weather ("We'd live here forever if we could"); sports ("the Super Bowl pre-game show is nine hours this year");and entertainment ("how many times have they re-made Titanic now?) Everyone enjoyed their dinners, except for the newlyweds, who felt some strange vibes coming from Calvin. JJ couldn't quite figure out why, but Rita had already put two and two together and spelled it all out for JJ later, as she spilled the beans about Kay.

Over the next two days, everywhere that JJ and Rita went, Calvin was sure to go. They crossed paths on the beach, in the lobby, at the pool. The greetings and questions seemed harmless on the surface, but when Calvin and Caroline started asking for mailing addresses and wanting to know what day they were leaving, the bells went off loud and clear.

"Calvin is no attorney, JJ." Rita advised. "He's from DC alright, but I'll bet you anything he's one of those undercover agents Kay told me about."

"Even if he is, he can't do anything here. We're not on U.S. soil," JJ explained.

"JJ, he's a United States Federal Agent. He could talk to the government here and have our plane stopped, or stop us at the gate next Saturday," Rita warned.

JJ gave Rita's argument some thought then replied, "You know what I think?"

"No, what do you think?"

"I think we got enough sun. Let's skip our dinner with them tonight, Mrs. Sherlock Holmes. Let's pack up, get to the airport, and get on the next flight home, now!"

"I love it when you like my ideas," Rita smiled. "We just out-smarted the whole United States of America!"

"Exactly what I was thinking," agreed JJ.

Calvin and Caroline didn't know what to think when they showed up for dinner that evening and there was no one in sight. Calvin checked for messages at the front desk and was shocked and dismayed when he was told that the Moultries had checked out that morning.

Just then, Roger and Suzie came running into the lobby from outside as Roger breathlessly apologized, "Sorry, we're late. Something came up. Where are JJ and Rita?"

"Checked out. Gone. This morning," Calvin advised.

Roger paused, shook his head, did an about-face and slowly headed back to the car that had just dropped them off. He leaned in and told the driver, who was wearing a uniform, a holstered gun and an Airport Security badge, "We're too late. They're gone."

The driver looked up and said, "Sorry to hear that, Agent Wilkins. Better luck next time."

Special Agent Roger Wilkins turned away and looked to the skies for the man who had gotten away once again on a wing and a prayer, and said, "That's it, buddy boy. You are d-u-n, done."

CHAPTER 25

CURTIS WAS BEHIND IN HIS classes at Kilmer. His family troubles back in Sugarfield translated into longer nights of hitting the books back in Evanston. Fortunately, he had a little help from his friends, who provided him with their class notes and lecture summaries.

Amber provided him with even more. On his first night back, the two of them made up for lost time with breathless greetings and murmurs of renewed longings, giving immeasurable new meaning to the old adage that "absence makes the heart grow fonder."

"I missed you, Curtis," whispered Amber into his ear, "is your family okay?"

"Yes they are," mumbled Curtis, into hers.

"I'm so happy to hear that," Amber breathed, "can you tell how happy I am?" as she gently kissed his ear, then his eyes, his nose and mouth.

"I think so," Curtis managed to reply, as he returned her kisses in the same locations and order. "Maybe you better tell me again."

"I said," Amber sighed, kissing his ear again, "I'm so happy," as she lightly slid over to his closed eyes, "to hear," as she slipped down to his nose, "that!" and finally settled onto his mouth.

After finally running out of available real estate, Amber curled up in Curtis' lap who had made himself comfortable in her overstuffed dorm room chair, and they savored their moment of intimacy in pure silence.

The spell was broken by Dayquan and his friend Gerald, as they burst into the room with news of renewed skirmishes on the Mexican border. This time they were determined to do something about it. This time they wanted to make their voices heard. This time they had to have a plan. Luckily, this time Curtis had news they could use. He was going to get them into the heart of the Republic. They were all going to Austin, Texas.

As Curtis explained to their hastily assembled group, he had been waiting for a phone call from his dad, which came today. He told them his dad was a Captain in McCall's Militia. His commanding officer was in Austin, and had great admiration for Jeb's recent actions in defense of their border. Curtis had asked his dad if he thought he could get their journalism group an audience with Colonel Maxwell Sloan of McCall's Militia for the purpose of enlightening the outside world about their immigration policies and practices.

At first, Col. Sloan didn't see the point, but upon reflection, he concluded that telling the story of what they were up against couldn't do any harm. On the contrary, it might gin up some additional support for their cause, particularly from some of the southern states who were already sympathetic with what the new Republic of Texas was trying to accomplish. When he was told that one of the interviewers would be Jeb's son, Curtis, that clinched it. The Colonel agreed to a half-hour interview in Austin the following Saturday.

Amber's excitable group couldn't be happier. They would now get a chance to do some real-life journalism concerning a huge ongoing international issue that few people had access to. The United States government had purposely avoided political contact with the Republic of Texas. They really had no insight into what was going on. This would be a big story. A real "scoop." Journalists had been know to write their own tickets after coming up with an exclusive like this. Maybe The Group would even be invited to come back! Think of that, sports fans! Ink-stained wretches of the world, rejoice!

May young people with fiery passions to change the
world never succumb to indifference.

One final detail remained. The interview was over the weekend, but traveling up and back by car would take a couple of days each way and some classes would have to be missed. Was Kilmer College up for the idea? Indeed, they were. The School of Journalism endorsed the off-campus interview and gave everyone who was involved time off for their "Field Trip." "Extra Credit" was being considered.

The next important decisions involved who was going on the trip - everyone! - who would come up with the questions - everyone! - and would actually ask the questions -Amber, because she was the leader; and Curtis, because he made it all happen. Everyone would take notes, and anyone could pass notes along if a follow-up question occurred to him or her in the process.

The road to Austin was paved with the best intentions. Amber's Journalism Appreciation Society couldn't wait for the opportunity to ask probing questions of the man who was leading the immigration charge at the border and was privy to all major decisions made in the Austin Presidential Mansion.

Colonel Maxwell Sloan was an adviser to President McCall's cabinet. He was a member of the War Department, which also included commanding officers from the Texas Rangers and National Guard. All former members of the United States Armed Forces had transferred into one of these units, giving the Republic of Texas a military force that was greater than Mexico's in numbers, skill and enthusiasm.

The War Department was chaired by Maj. General Wallace Newberry, a former U.S. Marine. He was considered to be a tactical genius, but he currently had his hands full amalgamating three different Texas military units into one disciplined fighting force. At this point, the Air and Army National Guard exhibited the best military bearing, followed by the Texas Rangers and then McCall's Militia, which was more like a posse that was thrown together to go after bad guys. There were a lot of free spirits in this group (which anyone who has ever been in the military knows is stamped out with an iron fist), and its actions were not always by the book. This had to change, and the General knew it. As hostilities were increasing along the Mexican border, this was no time for free-lancing.

In addition to the War Department, there were only three other cabinet positions, which was a streamlined version of the cabinets traditionally appointed by the President of the United States. Instead of forming 15 different departments with 15 different cabinet heads - another example of big, bloated, inefficient government - the cabinet of the Republic of Texas had only four. In addition to the War Department, there was a Secretary of State, a Secretary of the Treasury and an Attorney General. That was it. And that was the way George Washington did it, before dueling political parties were invented and self-serving political offices and appointments were created essentially to maintain the status quo.

Over time, the United States government grew heavy with party-line political positions and clashing, intractable views that infuriated the other side of the aisle and cast all hope of compromise to the winds. George Washington foresaw all of this when he said:

> *"Let me now warn you in the most solemn manner about the baneful effects of the spirit of the party. The continued mischief of the spirit of the party distracts from the public councils; agitates the community with ill-founded jealousies and false alarms; kindles the animosity of one party toward the other. In government purely elected, the spirit of the party is not encouraged."*

Ultimately, this is what led to the separation of Texas from the Union. As big as it was, Texas still wasn't big enough to hold two diametrically opposed political parties with two drastically different social agendas. Eventually, its more conservative base won out, and once again, the "Lone Star State" stood alone.

After three years of independence, its state of affairs was becoming more and more newsworthy as accusations of abortion clinic bombings and confrontations with Mexico grew and multiplied. The last thing the new Republic needed was to have another sensational front page story unfold on its very doorstep. Unfortunately, that story was only a day away.

Curtis had three passengers in his Mustang. Ken easily fit the remaining four in his old VW bus, making it a total of nine souls on the road to enlightenment. They left bright and early Thursday morning and kept up their chatter and enthusiasm for 10 hours straight. The Group agreed on three rooms at an economy motel in Memphis, Tennessee, right down the road from Graceland. Soon-Lee complimented Curtis on his knowledge of Elvis trivia, to which he replied in his deepest, most mellifluous voice, "Thank you very muh....!"

Quarters were tight at the motel because dollars were tight. Three people to a room, with two King Double Beds in each, would work, so long as someone didn't mind sleeping back-to-back with someone else, like many had to do when they were kids. Otherwise, they could thank Wayne for bringing along the inflatable mattresses.

Nobody felt like sleeping, so everyone crammed into Amber/ Soon-Lee/ Indira/ Joan's room for last-minute instructions and pizza. Amber went over the list of questions they all had prepared starting with the most important ones ("Why are you deporting immigrants and breaking up families?" "How can they become legal citizens?") and hoping to get to all of them pending any follow up questions and answers that might come up. Curtis would ask the questions he had personal knowledge about ("Could Hector Estrada and his wife be given special consideration, and be allowed to reunite with their daughter in Texas, considering the support Hector had given to Curtis' dad?")

When all suggestions - and bodies - were finally exhausted, they decided to call it a day. Amber reminded everyone that they would stick together as a group tomorrow, but not to emulate the mass media's practice of jostling for position and shouting out questions at will. They did not want to create the appearance of confrontation, but a confrontation is what it turned out to be, with tempers flaring and cameras rolling as world's collided on the steps of the sovereign nation's Capitol.

The Group of Nine knew they were in for a tough day when they turned on their TVs early the next morning. The reporter had sketchy details: "Late last night, an alleged band of roving gangs from Mexico attacked some ranchers in Mission, Texas. They returned fire and casualties were reported. Elements of the Texas Rangers are on the scene. We will keep you informed of further developments."

"Wow. Things are getting worse, aren't they?" concluded Dayquan. "Maybe we should call the whole thing off." "No way, Dayquan. We've come too far to turn back now," a visibly frustrated Curtis replied, as he went outside and began banging on doors. In a matter of minutes, everyone was out in the motel parking lot with their bags and opinions in hand. The chit-chat was put to rest when Amber spoke up and essentially said what Curtis said. "Obviously, this is going to make our job harder, but let's stick to the plan. We have an appointment with Colonel Sloan, and we're going to keep it. Let's go!"

Everyone piled into their designated vehicles and drove to the Capitol Building. As expected, the reporters and TV news crews were already set up on the Capitol steps questioning a senior government official who claimed to have no new information to report, and that someone would be making a statement later in the day. Also as expected, this didn't seem to satisfy the media or the general public, which had been slowly and fervently growing in numbers up and down the Capitol Square. They didn't have questions as much as they had answers of how to deal with the renegades at the border. Most of the shout-outs had to do with "taking them down," "picking them off" and "blowing them away."

Against this backdrop of ire and invective, the Kilmer College kids began making their way up through the crowd when Curtis suddenly spotted his dad, in full battlefield regalia, coming up the steps behind him. "Dad!" Curtis called out, as Jeb looked up and saw his son waving to him like a long-lost relative.

"Hey, Curt, partner! Fancy meeting you here!"

"Looks like you're here on official business," Curtis replied as he extended his hand, then nodded at his dad's camouflage uniform of the day.

"Yeah, we got a few things to straighten out. I don't know about your interview...." Jeb began, then abruptly stopped as he noticed the mini group that had assembled around the two of them. "So," Jeb changed course, "this is your group! A determined-looking outfit if I ever saw one," Jeb acknowledged, as he surveyed the cast of characters that looked like they had just come from Family Day at the United Nations.

"Yeah, we're eager beavers, alright," Curtis concurred, as he suddenly turned and motioned for Amber to step up for closer inspection. "Dad, this is Amber, our fearless leader. Amber, I'd like you to meet Captain Jeb Moultrie, my dad!"

"Oh my," Jeb replied. "Yes, indeed. I've heard all about you," exaggerated Jeb, totally taken aback by Amber's elegant ebony glow.

"Nice to meet you, Captain, I mean, Mr. Moultrie. Thank you for setting up our interview" Amber replied.

"You're welcome, Amber. Allow me to introduce my group to yours," as the Captain turned and invited his heavily armed militia squad up the stairs to say hello to Amber's warriors.

For the first time, Curtis caught sight of his next-door-neighbor, Frank, and JJ who were catching up with their comrades in arms. "Hey Frank," Curtis shouted, "here we go again, huh?" giving him a high-five in the process. "Never a dull moment, Curtis," Frank replied.

"Hey, bro!" Curtis blurted out as he gave JJ a fist bump and big bear hug. "I heard you had an interesting honeymoon in Jamaica!"

"Nothing I couldn't handle, little brother. Good to see you!" JJ answered, then turned his attention elsewhere. "And this must be Amber! I hope my little brother hasn't been giving you the wrong impression of our new Republic. We are basically very hospitable people"

"Okay...." Amber cautiously replied, observing the sea of unrest around her.

"We just have a little business to attend to at the moment," JJ explained.

"So do we," Amber countered, looking over at the Captain for support.

"Yes, well, things are a little chaotic right now, Amber, but I'll see what I can do," assured Jeb as he looked around for a higher authority.

"Here comes Colonel Sloan now," Jeb reported, and all eyes turned toward the senior officer of McCall's Militia, who was making his way through a phalanx of microphones, slowly ascending the Capitol steps.

When the Colonel was within earshot, Jeb called out, "Colonel Sloan! This way, sir!" His commanding officer nodded, then plodded through the last rank of reporters that stood between him and his right-hand man. Colonel Sloan stopped next to Capt. Moultrie, returned his salute and said, "Captain, we need to get inside for the briefing."

"Yes, Sir," Capt. Moultrie replied. "But first, do you suppose you could spend a couple of minutes with my son's college group? We scheduled an interview with them, remember?"

The Colonel looked at the multi-racial mix of young students with the impatience of a man heading into battle who is stopped and asked what all the fuss was about. "I'm sorry, but I don't think this is the time or the place..." Colonel Sloan began,

"But Colonel, that is precisely our point," Amber interjected. "Why has it come to this? Why are you prosecuting a war against immigrants? We were all immigrants once!"

"A few criminals do not represent an entire culture," Omar Muhammad followed up. "Why deny entry to everyone? Why deport the workers who are here. They are not the bad ones!"

Colonel Sloan had seen and heard enough and turned to continue his trek up the stairs. "Sorry," he said with finality. The TV crews had captured this exchange on camera and were ready to move to another set-up when they got caught up in the crush of the local citizens who had been listening in on this "debate" and began assailing the Kilmer Kids with questions of their own.

"Who are you, kid?" Who asked for your opinion?" "What do you know?"

Where are you from?" demanded another furious onlooker, as he spun Vince around and saw his college shirt...."Kilmer College? Evanston, Illinois?! Go home, ass hole!"

"Stop the war on immigration!" Omar yelled out again, trying to maintain his balance in the close quarters.

"Stop the deportation! Stop the hate", screamed Vince.

The first punch caught Vince squarely on the jaw and he went down like a ton of bricks. Curtis tried to play peacemaker and got himself punched in the gut for his efforts. The melee continued as the pushing and pawing escalated amid cries of "Stop the War," "Go to Hell," "Stop the Deportation" and "Screw you! Go back where you came from!"

The first sight of blood came from Dayquan. He was hit across the bridge of his nose and it instantly turned his face into red river valley. He stumbled and fell as Colonel Sloan shouted out orders for the Militia to come to the rescue of the writers-turned-fighters. And everything turned into a free-for-all.

Suddenly, the Moultries – Jeb, JJ and Curtis – found themselves in their own little back-to-back-to back circle, alternately trying to defend a kid, knock down an adversary or stop the fighting altogether. In the middle of all the mayhem, Amber tried to circle the wagons and protect her girls, but at this point no one was taking prisoners.

The steps of the Capitol Building were now swarming with dozens of lurching bodies and flaying arms. JJ and his men found themselves at war with their own Texas brethren as they tried to restore order. Shotgun reached for Amber's hand, who was still in protection mode like a mother hen. Big Frank picked up two participants at the same time and deposited them off to the side. Zeke caught a glimpse of Omar Muhammad tussling with one of the locals, then froze in a flashback of himself facing the enemy in Iraq.

Suddenly, a shot was fired. At first it was hard to tell where it came from. Pretty much all the local citizens in the crowd were "carrying." They always were, whether they were driving around town in their cars, chatting on the streets or going to a concert in the park. What used to be called "Second Amendment Rights" are now found in "Article One" of the new Republic of Texas Constitution. Around these parts, guns were as common as 10-gallon hats at a rodeo. At the first sound of gunfire, the 45s, 9 mils and Berettas came flying out of their holsters like Gary Cooper drawing down on bad man Frank Miller in High Noon. One happy trigger finger led to another, and a second shot rang out.

This deadly escalation caused McCall's Militia to draw their own side-arms, and on cue, they cordoned off the top of the stairs and fired a volley of shots into to the air to gain everyone's attention and terminate the violence.

After the flurry of gunfire had subsided, everyone paused and looked around. Some people who had been knocked down, were getting up. The Journalism majors were huddled together in a group on the Capitol steps. One was lying in a pool of blood. The air became silent except for the cries of Amber, who knelt down to get a closer look at Omar. She had no idea where the bullet had come from or where it had entered the body of Omar Muhammad, other than it had caused a lot of blood loss. Omar was unconscious, and Amber cried for help. A militia medic came rushing over. So did a civilian doctor who had been in the crowd. The medic ripped opened Omar's shirt, revealing a large, ugly chest wound. He attempted to staunch the blood flow with shirts off the backs of the onlookers.

Omar's eyes flickered open and when he saw Amber he haltingly asked, "Will we get the story now?"

Amber smiled down at him, brushed his hair aside and said "Yes, Omar, I promise you, we will get the story."

Omar smiled a soft smile, looked around at his friends and said, "That is good," then closed his eyes. The doctor who was taking Omar's pulse, lifted his fingers from Omar's neck and nodded from side to side. The silence was deafening, until the sobbing from the Kilmer students - and others - broke through the battle field pall.

As everyone tried to console one another, Soon-Lee came over and put her arm around Amber, leaving a trail of blood on her shoulder. "Soon-Lee!" Amber cried out, "You've been hit, too!"

"It is just my arm, Amber. See? This is not my worry," Soon-Lee explained, as she pointed to the person who was crouched over, forming his own pool of blood on the steps behind her. "He is!"

Amber looked at the man Soon-Lee was pointing to and saw that he was one of the local boys. It was Curtis Moultrie, of Sugarfield, Texas.

The ambulances and police vans had been summoned to the capital as soon as the hostilities began in anticipation of casualties such as those that occurred. The militia had helped the police round up the most egregious antagonists and arrested them. Medical personnel covered the body of Omar Mohammed, placed him on a gurney and wheeled him into an ambulance. Medics attended to Soon-Lee's arm wound and helped her into another ambulance. Curtis received the most attention, as doctors quickly examined his condition, wrapped his abdomen tightly, hooked up an IV and rushed him away in the hospital ambulance with lights flashing and sirens wailing.

No one had talked with Curtis. No one knew his condition. There were no other serious injuries to anyone else at the scene. Amber was still in shock. She sat silently on the Capitol steps staring off into the distance as Curtis' ambulance sped away. Capt. Jeb Moultrie was the first to break the spell. "All right men, the party's over. We will help the police disperse the crowd and establish a perimeter around the capital. Nobody gets through without authorization. When Col. Sloan gets his orders from the briefing inside we will get ours. That is all."

Jeb caught up with JJ and the two of them walked over to Amber and what was left of her group, sitting in a huddle on the Capitol steps. "Amber, I am so sorry about your friend," Jeb sympathized. "There is no excuse for what happened here."

"Everyone had guns," Amber vacantly replied. "We just came to talk, and now Omar is dead, Soon- Lee is hurt and who knows how Curtis is. Do you know? Is he hurt bad?"

"We don't know, Amber," answered JJ, "but we're going to find out. We're going to the hospital now."

"I'm going with you," Amber replied as she rose from the concrete steps and turned to her group, which was still dazed and confused. "Call your families and friends and tell them you are okay," Amber instructed. "Dayquan, you call Kilmer. You are in charge now. I will let you know about Curtis's condition as soon as I find out."

As the group was preparing to leave, a Police Department Capt. approached them and said "you will have to come with us to the station. We need your names and addresses. We have questions. You can make your calls from there."

The group looked to Amber, who looked to Jeb, who said a few words to the police officer then told Amber, "It's okay. They should go with the Captain. You can come with us."

The group solemnly followed the police and climbed into a van. Right next to them, six handcuffed, tattered citizens who were identified as being the key perpetrators of the Capitol riot were entering a second van. They glared over at the students, and the students defiantly glared back.

Amber was flanked by Jeb and JJ as she walked away from the scene of the crime and drove with them to a world of modern science and talented hands that all too often are put in the position of trying to save people from themselves. The emergency room doctors reported that Curtis had sustained a gunshot wound to his abdomen. There was some internal bleeding. He had undergone surgery and was currently in recovery. His condition was fair, but stable. Visitors would not be allowed until the next day.

Jeb and JJ decided to make the short 30-minute drive home to assure Jenny that everything was going to be all right. Jeb had had the foresight to call Jenny earlier and brief her on what had happened before Jenny would hear the breaking news of a student from Kilmer College being shot and killed in Austin. Amber told John and JJ that she would return to the motel where her friends were staying.

Instead, she called Dayquan and told him she was at the hospital, and that she would be staying there. All night.

CHAPTER 26

24 HOURS AFTER CURTIS HAD walked into a political buzz saw, Jeb, Jenny, JJ, Camilla and Jillian all arrived at the hospital to examine the toll it took on him. The receptionist at the front desk told them what room Curtis was in, but that only two visitors were allowed at a time.

Jeb and Jenny said they would go in first, but the receptionist said, "There is already one person in his room. Only one of you can go."

"One person?" asked Jeb. "Who?"

The receptionist replied, "A friend of the family," is what I was told.

"Who could that be?" Jenny nervously asked.

"Don't worry, dear. I'll go," Jeb firmly replied. "I'll find out who this friend of the family is." Jeb walked down the hospital corridor and found his son's room. He knocked lightly, went inside and found a groggy Curtis lying in bed, talking to his visitor, whom Jeb instantly recognized. He still had tubes in his nose, an IV in his arm and a big grin that turned up on his face when he saw his dad enter the room. Jeb leaned over the bed, gave his boy a very gentle hug and asked, "How you doing, partner?"

"I'm okay, dad. Really. A little tired, but I'll be up and out of here in time for dinner."

"I like your spirit, son, but there's no rush. You lost a lot of blood. You had surgery. When the doc says you can go, you'll go." Jeb turned his attention to his son's *fearless leader* and said "Hello again, Amber, how long have you been here?"

"All night," Amber replied. "I mean, I slept downstairs in the lobby all night. I just got here half an hour ago."

"I see," said Jeb, seeing things a lot more clearly now. "So you didn't go back to your motel."

"No," Amber replied. "I….couldn't. I called everyone this morning and told them Curtis is going to be fine."

Jeb nodded, then looked back down at his idealistic son. "You really took one for the team, didn't you? That's no surprise to me. You're always looking out for your friends and family. Now it's our turn to look out for you. Your mother, brother, sister and Jillian are all outside waiting to see you."

"I'll be leaving now," Amber said as she rose from her chair. "I feel so terrible about all of this Curtis."

"I have no regrets, Amber," Curtis replied, looking her straight in the eye. "None." Amber tearfully bent over Curtis' bed and whispered, "You get better now. I'll see you later," as she stroked Curtis' hand, smiled faintly at Jeb and left the room.

As Amber walked quickly past the front desk, the receptionist said, "All right, one more person can go in now."

"Who was that?" asked a startled Jenny.

"Oh, she's just one of the students from Kilmer," JJ answered. "One of the group." As thunderstruck as Jenny was, Jillian was doubly so. She didn't say a word. She didn't have to. There was something about this young woman. Something in the air…an impulse of energy that came and went as Amber did. She must be the charismatic African American leader that Curtis had told her about. He didn't tell her how beautiful she was. What else didn't he say?

Curtis' mother was the next person in the room. She tearfully embraced her courageous young son, and asked the questions that had kept her up all night: "What happened, Curtis? Who did this to you? How do you feel? When can you come home?"

"Well, mom," Curtis began, "somebody got angry with what our group was saying, there was some pushing and shoving, then somebody fired a gun - I don't know who - I got hit, but not bad, and like I told dad, I'll be home for Sunday dinner. Piece of cake! And that's probably what I'll have, too! Red Velvet cake. What do you think?"

"Curtis, be serious. You know this never would have happened if you didn't go to that school and join that group! When did you become a protestor? That's not who you are."

"Well, mom, in a way, I kind of am," Curtis said. "I think some of the things we're doing are wrong. I just can't sit around. I have to say something."

"And look what it got you," Jenny reminded her conscientious son.

"I don't care, mom. I believe in what I'm doing. Just like dad believes in what he's doing. And JJ, too."

"All I know is, *home is where the heart is*, sweetie."

"I'll be there mom, with bells on. And maybe a little bandage on the side."

"Oh Curtis, you're always joking!" Jenny said, with a smile. They *all* smiled at the truth in that statement, then Jeb took his wife's arm and said, "Let's go, dear. JJ and Camilla want to say hello, too." They gave their son a kiss and a hug, then stepped out of the room so that his brother and sister could step in.

All things considered, JJ was impressed. "Hey tough guy, you're looking good! You stood up for what you believed in out there. I respect that. I don't happen to agree with it, but I respect your right to say it.

"You sound just like Voltaire," Curtis replied.

"Volt-who??" asked JJ.

"The French writer from the 18th century. He said *I do not agree with what you say, but I will defend to the death your right to say it.* You guys are *so* alike!"

"Hey, college boy, don't give me any grief. I've got a brain, too, you know. You heard how I outsmarted the FBI down in Jamaica, didn't you?"

"I heard. I'd like to hear more."

"What's the FBI?" Camilla wanted to know.

"That's a whole other story," honey.

"I like stories!" Camilla reminded everybody.

"We'll talk about it on Sunday, okay? Curtis will be there, mom and dad will be there."

"And Jillian will be there…" Camilla reminded everybody once again.

"Jillian!" JJ shouted out. "She's waiting to see you! She's next! We better leave! See you, bro."

"Yeah… See ya……bro!" mimicked Camilla.

Then came Jillian. Curtis' long-time sweetheart entered his room with feelings of sadness and joy. She felt sad to see him lying there hooked up to tubes and monitors, his independent spirit now so dependent on others. She felt sad knowing he was going through life-altering experiences that she was not part of. She felt sad to think their relationship might never be the same.

She felt joy to see him lying there with a big smile on his face, holding his IV-restrained arms out as he greeted her. She felt joy knowing he was re-living all the wonderful times they had together in his mind. She felt joy to think their relationship was indestructible.

They were two conflicted souls, re-united on the meandering road through life. The moment their eyes met, they welled up with tears of sadness and joy. "Curtis, you look…good!" Jillian finally managed to say.

"I feel great! Now!" Curtis exuberantly replied. "Seeing you just lifted my spirits and put a song in my heart! Listen for yourself," as he directed her head toward his chest, giving him a better angle for the lengthy kiss he bestowed on her soft, sweet lips.

Jillian slowly recovered her senses and asked, "So how do you feel?"

"Do I feel any different," asked a grinning Curtis.

"No," answered a grinning Jillian. "They say maybe you can go home tomorrow."

"That's what they say and that's what I'm going to do!" verified Curtis.

"Maybe this isn't the time to ask, but are you going to continue with your journalism group?" Jillian asked anyway. "I mean look what happened to that poor boy from Pakistan."

"Omar," Curtis added. "He was such a smart, sweet guy. What a horrible thing to happen. Have they found out who did it? I remember some of those angry faces. I can help identify them. I'm not going to quit until they get the guy."

"Yes, I understand the police have some questions to ask you."

"And I'm ready to answer them. I'm not running away from this!"

"That's what I'm worried about, Curtis. When this is over, you don't have to be so involved, do you? You're one of us. You should be here."

"That's what mom said," answered Curtis. "There shouldn't be any *us* and *them*. That's the kind of gridlock we're trying to break through."

"When you say *we,* you mean Amber - was that her in here this morning?"

"Yes, it was."

"So what did you talk about?"

"She just wanted to know how I was doing. She blames herself for all of this. It's crazy. But she still thinks our mission is important."

"Do you? Are you going to continue with your....mission?"

"I don't see why not," Curtis replied.

"For one thing, Curtis, you see the risks involved. For another, while you're up there trying to create a more perfect world, we're having our own troubles down here."

"Like what?" asked Curtis.

"Like your dad's business," answered Jillian. "He doesn't say much, but we know things aren't going that well for him, or for anyone. Now your grandparents are living with them because they can't pay their medical bills. They had to sell their house. Our economy isn't so good. We're all having our financial problems."

"I guess I have been kind of preoccupied. I haven't been thinking about any of that."

"Maybe you should. We all miss you, Curtis. I miss you very much!"

"I miss you, too, pretty face," Curtis replied with a twinkle.

Jillian paused, then made the point they both had been trying to avoid. "It's up to you, Curtis."

"Yes," he slowly replied, averting his suddenly sorrowful eyes, "I know."

CHAPTER 27

ON ANY GIVEN NIGHT, FOREIGN intruders of various kinds can be seen – or heard – making their way across private Texas property in search of freedom or ill-gotten gains. Families who live in these areas are always on the alert, ready to defend themselves. On this particular evening, three ranchers on horseback who were returning from a day of mending fences, caught sight of a dozen individuals getting off an open truck and fanning out in different directions. This had all the earmarks of a being another batch of garden-variety illegal immigrants who were conned into paying what little money they had to a *coyote* who would take them across the border and set them free for as long as they could remain free.

Unfortunately, as the ranchers attempted to round them up, they realized that these individuals were more savvy than illegal immigrants, more desperate than slave traders and more cold-hearted than drug runners. These fly-by-night aliens were the worst of the worst: they were fugitives from Mexican prisons, and they were armed with anything but good intentions.

These chain gang refugees were bristling with machetes, Bowie knives and .38s and were prepared to go down in a blaze of glory before they would return to prison. They were out for conquests, gold and blood as they swarmed the Texas ranchers like buzzards on prairie dogs. They pulled one ranch hand off his horse and pummeled him until he was red and raw. One of the other ranchers got off a couple of shots and took down two convicts before he took a bullet in the back and slumped over in his saddle for the last and final time. The third rancher was pulled off his horse and sliced and diced like a Spanish onion, as the fight over who would take the man's mount waged on among the depraved desperados. By the time the dust had cleared, all the fugitives from justice had fled their would-be captors on foot or on horseback, leaving behind three of their own dead cellmates and three dead or dying ranchers.

It was like a mini Alamo, and it opened up old wounds throughout the new Republic. Pres. McCall wasted no time weighing in on television.

"My fellow Texans, as you undoubtedly know, last evening three Laredo ranchers were savagely attacked and killed by Mexican aliens. This isn't the first time peaceful law-abiding citizens of the great Republic of Texas have been brutalized by these lowlife pepper poppers. But it will be the last!

I have ordered the Texas Rangers and McCall's Militia to seek out and destroy these Mexican marauders. My orders are to shoot to kill. We will show no mercy and we will not rest until every dastardly coward tastes the justice of our rapid fire hollow points and Humvee cannons. Furthermore, additional units of our military are being deployed at every border crossing with the same orders to shoot to kill any and all individuals who attempt to cross our border illegally. I am ordering every citizen soldier to active duty to stamp out this uprising once and for all.

Let this be fair warning to the people and government of Mexico. Every citizen of our sovereign nation is prepared to take up arms to defend our land and our people from all enemies. Anyone who may be foolish enough to disregard this warning has a date with…The Peacemaker," Pres. McCall concluded as he picked up and waved his silver-plated Colt 45 at the camera.

Millions of unheard voices from every county in the country let out a roar of rage and support for their president and his no-nonsense plan. This would be the final warning that put the world on notice. This would be the final chapter. This would be the line in the sand that no one dared to cross. Until they did.

Hours later, as the patriotic fervor that was unleashed across the Republic began to subside, people began to consider how this would impact their lives. Jeb Moultrie was in the army now – for good. He would soon be receiving his orders from Col. Sloan, who would be receiving his orders from the Commanding General who had received his at the Capitol briefing that had taken place just two days earlier.

This would be a particularly difficult time for Jenny. The thought of her suddenly becoming a military wife – at her age – wasn't exactly what she thought they were signing up for in the beginning, only three short years ago.

In Jenny's mind, her parents would now have to be entirely in her care. Her mom could still help to a degree, but her dad was slipping into another world, fast. Jeb Jr. would be following in his dad's footsteps, as he always had, including leaving another war bride at home. Maybe she could move in, too. Maybe she wouldn't want to. Maybe she would *have to!* JJ wouldn't be here to keep his business running – neither would his dad. How would they pay their mortgages and their bills? Even a short-term deployment would set everybody back. Camilla would be okay. She was still young, but made of strong enough stuff to endure, thanks to her brothers and her parental upbringing. She also had her books and her friend, Maria, to turn to. Hopefully.

That could depend on what the Kazmarczyks decide to do. Is Frank up for another wild ride with the Moultrie clan - in the wild Republic of Texas? If he isn't, what happens to Maria? And what about Curtis? What will Curtis do? He could go back to school up north. His heart doesn't seem to be in the fight we are having down here. Especially considering what just happened to him. The good news is, he's coming home tomorrow. We'll talk it over. We'll see. He's got a mind of his own, we all know that.

"I wonder what he's thinking," Jenny thought aloud, "about a lot of things." She reflected for a moment on all the recent events that had befallen their family and their nation and asked herself one final question: "What else could possibly go wrong?" The answer came that evening.

"Ladies and gentlemen," the television voice solemnly intoned, "the President of the United States." The TV screen dissolved from the great presidential seal to President Melanie Roberts Simpson, sitting behind her desk in the oval office with the Stars and Stripes standing tall over her right shoulder. She wore a dark blue pants suit with a small American flag on her lapel, a silvery satin blouse and opal vintage earrings and pendant set in sterling silver. Her pleasant, confident demeanor was further reflected in the photograph on her desk of herself, her husband and her daughter playfully interacting with some young African children in their native land. She folded her hands and immediately got to the point.

"Good evening, my fellow Americans. I am speaking to you tonight to address the concerns I know you have, and I have, regarding the recent violent events that have transpired in the Republic of Texas, and what we will be doing to protect our interests and our people.

As you know, three years ago the state of Texas was allowed to separate from the United States of America and reclaim its status as a sovereign nation. The Supreme Court ruled that the annexation of Texas in 1845 was in violation of the United States Constitution. In order to annex a sovereign nation, which Texas was at the time, a two-thirds vote of Congress would have been required. This vote was never taken.

Therefore, technically, Texas was never a state, and in 2007, the people of Texas affirmed their desire to remain a sovereign nation by majority vote. Furthermore, the high court pointed out that when the people feel their rights are not being secured by their government, "it is the right of the people to alter or abolish it and to institute new government," as is stated in the Bill of Rights.

Regardless of the arguments that are still ongoing today, The Republic of Texas is currently an independent nation. However....per the terms of separation....the Republic of Texas agreed to not interfere with the governance of the United States, the rights of its people or its allies. But in point of fact, they have violated every one of those agreements.

Over the past few months there has been a fatal bombing of an abortion clinic in the state of Oklahoma, which we have been unable to fully investigate because a person of interest is a Republic of Texas citizen and we have not been allowed to question him or extradite him. Recently, there was a shooting on the steps of the Capitol in Austin, Texas in which a Pakistani student from a college in Illinois was killed. Again, we have not been allowed to investigate this murder and the government of Pakistan is pressing us to do so. Finally, recent incidents of shootings and killings near the Mexican border have resulted in a heightened threat of military retribution by the Republic of Texas.

None of these actions is acceptable. And they must cease. If our diplomatic efforts to investigate the killings of Americans and foreign students continue to be spurned, we will resort to other measures. Similarly, we will not tolerate any military action at the border. Mexico is a trading partner of ours, and our working relationship with them at the California, Arizona and New Mexico borders is good. Toward that end, I have federalized the National Guard from those states and put them on high alert.

However, the door is still open for cooperation on these matters. I hope this invitation is accepted. The alternative is not something anyone should want to engage in…ever again. Thank you, good night and God Bless the United States of America."

As the screen faded to black, visions of confrontations danced in the heads of millions of agitated, partisan people. And the shot heard around the world was yet to come.

CHAPTER 28

CURTIS' HOMECOMING WASN'T ANYTHING LIKE his father's. When Jeb came marching home from his heroic incident at the border, the Moultrie front yard was packed with well-wishing friends and neighbors in a band shell of patriotic music, banners and salutes.

This time it was different. This time, only Jeb and JJ stood by the curb as the Medi-Van pulled up in front of the house. After the EMTs carefully downloaded their wheel-chair bound passenger, Curtis' father and brother greeted him with a series of high-fives and fist bumps, then got behind him for the short ride to the front porch and an extra-special family reunion.

Before you could say, "Good Golly, Miss Molly," the Curtis Moultrie fan club burst out the front door and made a beeline to their recovering idol. Camilla was the fastest out of the gate and jumped into Curtis' lap before anyone could stop her. "Hey Squeaky, give me a little breathing room, would you? I've got a story to tell you about the biggest Ferris Wheel in the whole world!" "I want to hear it! Three times!" Camilla pleaded.

Jenny and Jillian were next. "It's so wonderful to see you home again, son, where you belong. Don't you ever scare me like that again!"

"Okay, I promise. I'll never scare you like that again, Mom. Until Halloween!"

"Oh Curtis," Jenny exclaimed, "what am I going to do with you?"

"Exactly my question," Jillian echoed, grasping Curtis' hand with both of hers.

"Anything you like, petunia face," he answered, looking up into her glowing visage and adding his other hand to the bonding process. "Anything at all."

Their laser-locked eyes resurrected the pathway that had led to each other's hearts in simpler times, a pathway now strewn with obstacles and fears. But a pathway nonetheless. And it was beckoning.

Curtis snapped out of his trip down memory lane long enough to ask, "And how are grandma and grandpa Taylor? We can't have a party without them!"

"They're good," Jeb answered. "They're inside. They can't wait to see you!"

"Then let's roll, people!" Curtis commanded. "I have miles to go before I sleep!" "Are you sure he's alright, dad?" JJ whispered to his father, "or is that something else from...*Voltaire?*"

Jeb stared blankly at his son for a second and then said, "Volt-who?"

From The Taylors' viewpoint, their notorious grandson looked about as chipper as a bird that had fallen out of its nest could possibly look, and they were still at a loss over the whys and wherefores of his recent Capitol appearance.

"Exactly what is it that you are studying in school, Curtis?" grandma Taylor wanted to know.

"Journalism, grandma Taylor. I'm learning how to write stories about the things people do."

"And you brought your whole class down here for that? Aren't there people in the north that you could be writing about?"

"Yes, but there are a lot more interesting things going on down here right now, and people want to know more about them."

"Are we that different from everyone else, Curtis?"

"In some ways, yes. That's what makes it so interesting. Different people see the same thing in different ways. I just want to be there, taking notes. That's what a journalist does," Curtis explained with finality.

"Draw! You lily-livered polecat!" grandpa Taylor shouted out.

"Grandpa's been watching a lot of old cowboy movies, lately. He loves those days," his devoted wife explained.

"Don't worry, grandpa. You're still the fastest gun in the west!" assured his grandson.

"From my cold, dead hand!" Gramps warned, shaking his fist in defiance.

"Dinner's ready!" Jenny called out. "Come and get it!" Like a moth to a flame, the famished family flitted and darted around the dining room table, ogling and praising the bill of fare, until Jeb ordered the troops to stand behind their chairs for a moment of silence in memory of the young man who was killed and the others who were hurt when idealism and reality crossed swords on the steps of the Texas capitol.

The commemoration was followed by a recitation of Grace which was followed by a glorious meal and a meaningful conversation which took on a far more serious tone than anyone in the Moultrie home had ever remembered hearing.

Initially, Curtis did most of the talking. He began at the beginning and described what life was like on the Kilmer College campus, the kinds of courses he was taking and the camaraderie that quickly developed among his merry band of journalism junkies.

Mom asked how the food was. "Generally okay," Curtis answered. "You get the usual bacon and eggs or cereal for breakfast, sandwiches or pizza for lunch and meat and potatoes dinners with sliced beef, chicken, meatloaf, or pork chops and the occasional *mystery meat* which everyone has tried to identify but failed miserably.

Mom, when I tell everyone the kind of meals you prepare on a daily basis their mouths start watering like a dog begging for a fresh bone. Your pecan pies are a high point of our journalism meetings and if my writing career turns out to be a pipe dream, I'll open up a *Jenny's Original Pecan Pies* franchise up there and make you more money than a Texas oilman!"

Dad asked how well he got along with everyone. "Real well," Curtis answered. "I'm kind of like the missing piece in the jigsaw puzzle. It makes the picture complete. Vince says I talk kind of funny, but then he's from Brooklyn, you know? And you should hear Omar," as Curtis suddenly realized he was talking about his fallen friend, he started over, "I mean you *should* have heard Omar. His English wasn't great, but his ideas were. The same with Soon-Lee and Indira. It's the thought that counts, right? I mean we're like a family there. Kind of like us, minus any lunatic people like JJ."

"Hey, college boy, don't go pushing your luck," advised JJ. "I'll let that one pass 'cause you're on Injured Reserve. When you're ready to play again, I'll knock you down a peg or two. Speaking of which, are there any good teams up there? What do you do for fun?"

"Yeah JJ, I went to a Kilmer football game. We lost 42 to 7. It's not a big sports school. But there's a lot going on in Chicago!"

"Like what?" JJ asked. "Like museums, the aquarium, the planetarium, Navy Pier. That's where the Ferris wheel is, Camilla. It's huge!"

"Did you go on it?" asked Camilla.

"Sure did! Many times, Squeaky."

"With who?"

"Oh," Curtis managed to reply, "with friends from school. Different people."

"Was it more fun than our Ferris Wheel, Curtis?" asked a very interested Jillian.

"Oh yeah, I mean *absolutely not*! How could it be? You weren't there."

"No, I wasn't there. Maybe I should come up and visit."

"Well, maybe you should. Sure!"

As Curtis struggled to regain control of the conversation, the doorbell rang. "Saved by the bell," thought Curtis. "I wonder who that could be?" thought JJ, as his mind rushed back to the family dinner that was so rudely interrupted by the investigative TV reporter weeks ago.

"I'll get it!" Camilla shouted out as she rushed to be the one to open the door once again, only this time she came back to announce a different surprise visitor.

"There's somebody to see you, Curtis."

"Who?"

"It's Amber," Camilla said, as the blood drained from Curtis' face. "And her friends," added Camilla, as the color returned to Curtis' cheeks which suddenly dimpled into a big grin.

Curtis wheeled himself to the front door and invited his friends to come inside. Amber presented a striking figure in her ¾-length baby blue tailored jeans and white sleeveless top, with a red bandana knotted loosely around her neck and jet black hair pulled back from her elegant ebony features. She bent over and wrapped her arms around Curtis in a lengthy embrace, then looked up into a sea of expressionless faces, most notably the crackling stare down emanating from Jillian.

Curtis stated the obvious, "Everybody...I think you know Amber." Everybody knew and everybody nodded.

"I hope we're not intruding," Amber said. "We are on our way back to Illinois and wanted to see how Curtis was doing before we left."

"I'm glad you did," Curtis replied. "Come on in!" As the far-from-home students entered the Moultrie home, Curtis introduced his family. "This is my mom, dad, brother JJ and his wife, Rita, my sister, Camilla, my grandparents and my friend, Jillian." Then he introduced the group individually. "This is Dayquan, Amber's second-in-command and long-time friend from Michigan; Soon-Lee, our wounded warrior from China; Indira from Calcutta, India; and Vince, Wayne, Al, Ken and Joan from the States."

There were smiles and handshakes all around, then Curtis' group gathered around him amid a flurry of questions: "How are you feeling?.... (Good, better every day); do you know what happened at the Capitol?.... (Not yet, they're working on it); When will you be coming back to school?...(We'll see); Will we ever get any interviews with anyone?...(Not at this time. Most everyone has been deployed somewhere or other)."

When Jeb and Jenny saw the concern and affection everyone had for their son, they couldn't help but feel good about the new world he had become part of and how he had earned their respect. Jeb immediately told everyone to make themselves at home and Jenny announced that she still had some leftovers if anyone was interested. She was instantly taken up on her generous offer and soon everyone congregated around the dinner table and kitchen table and began finishing off the remaining specialties of the house with gusto and gratitude.

Anyone who might have come across this scene would have thought they had stumbled onto an international cooking convention of foreign dignitaries who were comparing descriptions of various dishes and desserts as they carried their plates throughout the house.

"That is Cottage Pie," explained Jenny to a satiated Wayne. "It's ground meat with onions, garlic, and tomatoes and mashed potatoes spread on top. The Red Eye gravy on the ham slices is made with coffee, Joan! Yes, coffee!

Glad you liked the Pear Lime Salad and Mississippi Mud Cake, Al. My mother taught me those!"

The impromptu Meet & Greet had its moments. JJ hit it off talking sports with Ken and Wayne. "Where do you think the term Friday Night Lights came from, boys?" JJ remarked for the umpteenth time. Dayquan tried discussing the history of discriminatory practices of the world with a polite but noncommittal Jeb. Indira was having a one-way conversation with grandma Taylor until she took out her wallet and showed her the picture of her own grandmother. And the ice was broken.

Soon-Lee was fascinated by Camilla's reading skills and appreciation of books. All the while, Amber was working the room, dropping in and out of conversations, then lingering over Curtis' wheelchair long enough to whisper sweet somethings into his ear and receive a reply in the same fashion. Jillian never took her eyes off of her, and whispered comments of her own to JJ's bride, Rita. They both shared the same perspective on this woman's obvious magnetism and charms, and vowed to head off any further advances.

Before any deeper conversations or actions could be misinterpreted, Curtis signaled the end of the proceedings with a toast. He thanked all his friends for coming, and then offered one final salutation as he raised his water glass on high: "May we live in interesting times!"

"Alright, that does it!" responded a frustrated JJ. "I know what that is, Curtis. That's *Voltaire!*" As everyone turned toward JJ with uncertain smiles, Curtis looked at his hopeful brother, shook his head from side to side and said, *"Confucius!"*

Before JJ could register a complaint, grandpa Taylor ceremoniously rose from his chair and said, *"May the good Lord take a likin' to you."* As all heads swiveled back to grandpa's location, he added, *"Roy Rogers!"*

And the walls came tumbling down with laughter and good cheer.

After the guests had left and everyone had helped with the dishes, Jeb motioned for his celebrated son to join him for a private conversation. "So, Curtis, tell me what is going on with you and Amber?"

"Nothing's going on, dad. We're just good friends."

"It's more than that, son. I can tell, so can everyone else tell. Jillian can see it, too."

"Well, maybe I do have some personal feelings for her," Curtis admitted. "We have some kind of connection."

"Great! My son goes off to college and immediately falls for a rabble-rouser; an African American rabble-rouser!"

"She's not a rabble rouser, dad. She and I happen to believe in the same things."

"How can this happen?" a pacing Jeb persisted.

"I don't know, dad. Things happen. It turns out I've become good friends with Dayquan, too. And he's gay!"

"What?! Now your buddy-buddy with a black gay guy? I knew there was something strange about him, getting all emotional talking about fairness for *all* types of people! Curtis, what the hell are you thinking?"

"It's the world we live in, dad."

"It's not the world *I* live in."

"I know that, dad, but times are changing. You have to be open-minded."

"Hey, I'm as open-minded as the next guy, but there is a limit. You've got to stand for something!"

"You can't control human nature dad. People are who they are."

"And just who are you, son? Are you still a Moultrie, and I don't mean in name only?"

"I'll always be a Moultrie. This is just me, branching out."

"We'll, just don't forget your roots while you're busy branching out. It's going to be tough holding this family together now that JJ and I are being deployed, you know."

"I know. I've been thinking about that dad, and I've decided to hold down the fort while you're gone."

Jeb paused for a moment then began to ask for clarification, "You mean?…"

"Yes, I'm not going back to Kilmer," Curtis verified. "I'm going to stay home. I already called the school and told them that by the time I come back I will have missed too many classes to complete the term. They understood and said they would hold my scholarship for me."

Jeb paused again, then apologetically proceeded, "Well, Curtis I don't know that I can ask you to do that."

"It's a done deal, dad. You can count on me!"

Jeb gave his son a long hard look follow by a long firm hug as the two of them reconciled their differences at that very moment.

As they headed back towards the living room, Jillian crossed their path and asked if she could steal Curtis for a minute. Both men knew what was coming, and neither looked forward to it.

"Your friends are nice," Jillian began. "They were very attentive to you."

"Yes, they are. And they were."

"Especially Amber, I thought," Jillian elaborated.

"She's just a super friendly person," Curtis acknowledged.

"Uh-huh, Jillian coolly replied. "I couldn't help but notice that red bandanna she was wearing. It looked a lot like the one you gave me."

"Oh that, well, yes I gave it to her as a present."

"Really? What kind of present," Jillian asked, her temperature rising.

Then Curtis applied the stunner. "It was a going-away present. I won't be seeing her again. I decided to drop out of Kilmer and stay home."

Jillian could have been knocked over with a feather. "You're staying home?"

"Yes, for three important reasons. I want to try to keep dad's and JJ's businesses going while they're gone, and I want to help mom around the house."

"You're serious?"

"Absolutely. I told Amber and dad tonight."

Jillian processed what she was hearing with joy and trepidation, then moved on to the reason she was waiting to hear: "And what's the third reason you're staying home, Curtis?"

"It's the *first* reason, really. And I'm looking right at her."

In that moment of compassion, selflessness and love, Curtis cleared Jillian's mind of all doubts and fears she had been harboring about the direction his life – and their relationship - was heading. Hearing that it was all heading home made her feel like a young girl at a county fair coming home with a kewpie doll on one arm and a young man who had just promised his undying love on the other.

"Home at last," Jillian thought as a current of warmth and serenity rushed throughout her body. "We are home at last!"

CHAPTER 29

THE FOLLOWING MORNING, JEB AND Jeb Jr. put on their camouflage fatigues, said a quick, military-like farewell to their tearful families and asked Curtis to drive them to the Houston Motor Pool, where Capt. Moultrie relayed the orders he had received from Col. Sloan.

"Operation Bushwacker" was divided into two phases. Half of Jeb's unit was assigned Humvees for their mission to seek out and destroy the fugitives who had so ruthlessly butchered the Laredo ranchers. They were given a specific sector to search which was adjacent to sectors that other militia units had under surveillance. It was a coordinated *pincers* movement which would leave the fugitives with no way to escape.

Jeb, JJ and Zeke would be returning to the border to reinforce the National Guard in Humvees of their own, only these were outfitted with heavier armaments, including a 40-millimeter Grenade Machine Gun and 30-millimeter cannon. These colossal war machines were capable of blowing boats out of the Rio Grande and trucks off the roadways from great distances. The time had come to make some examples of people, and the orders to Shoot First and Ask Questions Later were greeted with nods of approval from every soldier, especially from Zeke, the Post Traumatic Stress-afflicted Iraqi war veteran who thought he saw the face of the enemy in every crowd. Capt. Moultrie knew he would have to keep an eye on him.

"Operation Bushwacker" bagged three fugitives on the first day.

Following a trail of highway robberies of money, guns and automobiles, the Humvees of Sector Two laid in wait for the runaway convicts as the Humvees of Sector One got on their tail and opened up with their onboard 3-barrel Gattling Gun and Recoilless Rifle. In the resulting ambush, the Humvees of Sector Two pounded them with their own M101 Howitzer, sending the band of misfits and their vehicles to kingdom come in a crossfire of bullets and rockets that would have made Gen. Sam Houston proud.

The next day, a couple of strays on the run were picked off by militia sharpshooters, and the remaining gangsters were jettisoned off their horses with a Humvee 20-millimeter cannon that meted out justice with the finality of a baseball bat cracking open a pinata.

At the same time, Capt Jeb Moultrie was enjoying some target practice of his own as his crew opened up on unidentified water craft speeding across the Rio Grande, sending everyone aboard sky high in a torrent of shrapnel and pixie dust. Trucks and vehicles that did not obey orders to stop were routinely peppered with automatic fire and reduced to a pile of rubble. If this wasn't a war, it was basic training. And the militia men remained on high alert. The eyes of Texas were on the dangerous, undesirable foreigners at the Mexican border.

Unfortunately, the eyes of the most vicious foreigners anyone had ever seen were on Houston.

The only McCall's Militia man who was not present - but accounted for – during these engagements was Frank Kazmarczyk. As Jenny and others had anticipated, Frank and Emma had seen enough. Frank was an aerospace designer, not a fighter. He had helped JJ and Jeb because he could, but becoming a full-time soldier was not in the cards for him or for Emma. They both knew they had done all they could.

As much as Emma still felt some obligation to the parents and children of Sugarfield, she also believed she was leaving behind a better learning environment than existed when she had gotten there. Emma felt a genuine sense of accomplishment, knowing that her answers to her students' questions raised additional questions in their minds. It was the ongoing educational process of intellectual involvement, rather than simple rote learning, that she was striving for.

Frank had no regrets about resigning from the militia or from his job. He had gotten his feet wet in difficult aeronautical design challenges and improbable rescue missions, and he didn't see himself making a career of the latter.

Now it was time to go. The only remaining question – and it was a big one – was "What would happen to Maria?" There was still no word on the possible return of Maria's parents, though her father's support of Capt. Jeb Moultrie on the Mexican side of the border had been duly noted by the Republic of Texas.

Maria's only hope resided next door. Camilla had offered to share her room with her best friend and fellow book reader. She argued her case with everyone in the house, and while her mom was "thinking it over," Camilla heard from the most influential person in the family. One night at dinner, grandma Taylor spoke up and said, "I think we should invite Maria into our home. She is a kind and compassionate girl."

That about-face was the clincher. Maria packed up her clothes, her books and her Bible and took her place at the Moultrie table between an exuberant Camilla and a forgiving grandma Taylor.

As different as things seemed at home when Curtis had returned from the calamity at the Capitol, they seemed doubly different now. His mom had her hands full. Looking after her parents' medical and personal needs was nearly as time-consuming as running the house. And living on a military budget was proving to be impossible. Jenny was forced to dip into their savings to stay afloat. Somehow, she managed to still put in 20 hours a week at her job with the home health company, knowing that every little bit helped.

Maria was another mouth to feed, although Jenny had no compunctions about making that decision. Her daughter-in-law, Rita, decided to stay in her own home and was working full-time, trying to keep up with their mortgage payments. Depending on how long the deployment lasted, they might be forced to sell their house and move in…where?

Rita's parents had moved into a small "efficiency" apartment. Over at the Moultrie place, grandma and grandpa Taylor were using JJ's room. Maria was with Camilla in hers, and Curtis was back in his old room. Thank God, Curtis was back in his old room!

The kid from Kilmer was doing everything in his power to keep the family together and semi-solvent. He was not a builder like his dad, but he had learned a thing or two from him back when he had helped with some of the more routine projects. Curtis tried to pick up where his dad left off. He could swing a hammer and do some basic carpentry, but he had to hire handymen to do the plumbing and electrical work in order to keep up with the few odd jobs left on his dad's docket.

Keeping JJ's landscaping business going was a lot easier to do, and a lot harder to do at the same time, especially when he spent half the day behind the fumes and roar of a power mower. He could also handle the lawn trimming, edging and power washing that came with the territory until he literally and figuratively ran out of gas, at which point he would call in JJ's otherwise-out-of-work helpers. At the end of the day, Curtis hit the sheets like a man coming home from a 50K marathon for the first time in his life.

Curtis was his family's rock. There is no telling how they would have survived without him. In quiet moments of clarity, he would compare and contrast – as they like to say in school – the life he had at Kilmer College and the reality he had been thrust into at home. At Kilmer, and hopefully later in life, he could be an idea man, a creative man, a writer. He could do the big picture stuff. And if he turned out to be good at it, people would listen to him. And pay him!

Here at home, he was obviously - and painfully - more hands-on. And while there is something to be said for cutting the perfect miter joint or planting a tree, Cutis concluded he would be better off using his cerebral cortex rather than his dad's power table saw. He looked forward to returning to campus life as soon as the feuding and fighting between irresistible forces and immovable objects came to an end, or at least ratcheted down to a low roar and everyone could get on with their lives.

What would it take for that to happen, he wondered:

A - A meeting of the minds?
B - A stalemate?
C - A vanquished enemy?
D - An act of God?

The correct answer is written deep in the heart of Texas.

CHAPTER 30

THE THREE MEN WERE INSEPARABLE. They had grown up together and moved to Channelview, Texas a year ago. Everyone was used to seeing Javier, Sami and Mikhail going to work, shopping and driving around town. They always said "Hello," but otherwise kept to themselves in their shared apartment.

On this particular day, they drove over to Lynchburg and got on the Houston Ship Channel Ferry to La Porte, Texas which is the site of the San Jacinto State Park, a popular tourist attraction. The ferry carries passengers, bicycles and automobiles and was filled to near capacity as the three close friends drove their SUV onto the boat, then got out to see the sights as they had done many times before.

They were very familiar with the Houston Ship Channel, inasmuch as they had often viewed it from the observation deck of the San Jacinto Monument, the primary feature of the park. It was here that the decisive battle of the Texas Revolution was fought. On April 21, 1836 Gen Sam Houston's Texas Army defeated Gen Antonio Lopez de Santa Anna and the Mexican Army in the Battle of San Jacinto. Three days later, Gen Santa Anna signed a peace treaty that directed the Mexican Army to leave the region and recognized the Republic of Texas as a sovereign nation.

Ever since then, thousands of proud Texans had come to this place to visit the museum and re-live that historic moment. Javier, Sami and Mikhail had come for the view.

The Houston Ship Channel is the key to Houston's status as a major international shipping port. It runs for over 50 miles from the eastern edge of the city of Houston to the Gulf of Mexico. It is continually being widened and deepened by dredging to accommodate larger and larger ships, tankers and barges. There are numerous terminals along the way, including ports for cruise ships, and dozens of private docks for many industries, especially oil refineries.

This was the dock that the three amigos had their eye on for the last six months. And this was the dock they had every intention of arriving at today. They had gone over their plan a hundred times in their apartment and made many dry runs on the ferry. Today would be the real thing. Today they would do irreparable harm to a nation of arrogance, ruthlessness and false pride. Today they would strike a blow for the oppressed.

Halfway across the Channel, Javier and Sami headed up to the ferry's unguarded bridge. As the captain turned around to see who was joining him, he felt the sting of Sami's silenced Ruger and was dead before he hit the floor. A crewman who was also present instantly met the same fate.

Javier took the big wheel and changed course to a heading that lined him up with the oil tanker that was taking on refined crude at the dock directly ahead. By this time, some of the passengers were aware of the course change and began looking around for an explanation. What they saw were three frantic deck hands scurrying around the boat, heading up towards the bridge. They stopped in their tracks when they saw Sami standing at the top of the stairs aiming an AK-47 in their direction.

Everyone jumped for cover as rapid-fire shots rang out and shards of wood, metal and glass began flying around indiscriminately like a fireworks display gone awry. Javier stayed true to his course as he closed in on the gigantic target before him. The rampaging off-course ferry caught the attention of dock workers who were pointing and gesturing wildly, having just put two and two together. Warning sirens sounded and Channel Police boats were hurriedly dispatched to the scene.

On board the commandeered ferry, a few of the passengers suddenly realized the imminent danger and prepared to storm the bridge. Eight men answered the call and armed themselves with the boat's fire extinguishers and fire axes. They began throwing life jackets up at the lone sentry as a sort of flak in advance of their hastily planned attack. The self-appointed leader of this enraged party of patriots yelled out, "Let's Roll!" and they stormed the bridge like it was a pill box on Iwo Jima.

The two men who went first never went anywhere without their side arms, and began popping away at the perp at the top of the stairs with a vengeance, but they were no match for the automatic fire.

One was cut down before he got half way up the stairs, and the second Texas volunteer was nicked but returned the favor before he fell. The remaining attackers struggled to gain ground and finally fell back to the deck below. While all this was going on, Mikhail was all alone at the front of the boat inside his blacked-out SUV.

It was tightly packed with enough explosives to blow up a city block, and it was surrounded with 500 gallons of gasoline for good measure. Mikhail set the timer on the improvised bomb to go off when he hit "Send" on his cell phone. He exited the vehicle and went outside to the bow of the boat. He signaled Javier in the wheelhouse that the deal was ready to go down, as all the remaining passengers began jumping ship. Less than a minute later, Javier was hit by machine gun fire from the Channel Police and slumped over the wheel to which he had tied himself, Sami stood up on top of the bridge facing the approaching doomsday tanker with his arms raised in victory, and Mikhail sent the message to end all messages.

The explosion reverberated throughout Houston like a space shuttle liftoff. Raging red, super-hot flames shot up instantly, forty feet into the air, leaping over the sleeping force-fed tanker and onto its deck where the refined oil fumes and solvents play. It was a marriage made in Hell, and its explosive consummation produced evil curls of thick black smoke mingled with fire and brimstone in an inferno even Dante could never imagine.

The living, breathing blaze backed up through refinery pipelines and touched off shrieking new explosions as oil tanks and reservoirs fell like dominoes. Refinery towers melted in a searing, scalding bath of white heat generated by the combined conflagration of liquefied petroleum gasses, kerosene and jet fuel. Hundreds of acres of refined energy had become a minefield of death and destruction, laying waste to all who had held it so dear.

The blaze raged on for hours. First Responders couldn't get close enough to the inferno to be of much help to anyone, other than the few workers who were thrown clear of the flames by the initial concussive blast. Safety vales had automatically shut down some refinery operations, thereby saving some infrastructure, petroleum products and lives.

Fire departments from all over Houston threw everything they had at the fire, then established a perimeter to keep the groping flames from reaching out for more fuel to feed its ravenous appetite. Helicopters dropped fire-suppressing agents from above, and 36 hours after the ferry boat torpedo slammed into a slumbering oil guzzler, the fire was struck.

The refinery employed 450 people and half of them were unaccounted for. Millions of gallons of oil had spent its energy on the masters of its evolution, and the entire Republic of Texas went ballistic. The world hadn't witnessed anything so depraved and indifferent since 9/11. And like 9/11, the reaction was swift and severe.

One day after the fact, President Jefferson McCall shouted out his defiance to a national TV audience as he stood in front of the smoldering pile of rubble that had once been his pride and joy.

"Never in the 160-year history of the Republic of Texas has our sovereign nation been so ruthlessly and savagely attacked. The lives and industry that lie smoldering on this sacred land will be avenged. The perpetrators will be rooted out and executed by the terrible swift sword of God's justice.

This act of terrorism and cowardice emanated from the country of Mexico, a land that we soundly defeated in battle over 150 years ago, practically on this very spot. Apparently, they did not get the message! Well, now hear this!

I am giving President Jose Obrigon of Mexico 24 hours to produce the cartel that is responsible for this unprovoked attack on the Republic of Texas. Otherwise, I will assume that President Jose Obrigon of Mexico is personally responsible for this atrocity. And we will come for you. We will fight fire with fire. We will come by land, by water and by air and we will destroy your factories and your way of life as you have destroyed ours. We will permanently close our border, after we have sent all illegal aliens back to Mexico where they will remain forever.

You will never know what hit you. Our military power will easily overwhelm whatever meager resistance you may assemble, as we have done in the past. I promise you, President Obrigon, this unconscionable action will not go unpunished. You have 24 hours to turn over the responsible cartel, or we will come for them. And for you!"

The wheels of war were in motion. Everything President McCall had outlined was being implemented. The Militia's Humvees were being re-outfitted and their crews were being re-supplied. The jet aircraft of the Air National Guard were being armed with machine gun ammunition and rockets. The Texas Rangers and infantry troops were massing at their headquarters to go over comprehensive, coordinated, battle plans. Drones were being programmed and armed.

Then came the promises of additional support. The governors of the states of Alabama, Louisiana and Mississippi offered to place their National Guard units on alert, ready to back up the Texas military if and when it was deemed necessary. This immediately brought up the question in some quarters of whether or not individual states could enter active duty in support of Texas. While it didn't seem likely that they could, the three governors claimed that their "States Rights" allowed them to do whatever was necessary to protect their own interests. If elements in Mexico could attack Texas, could Mississippi, Alabama or Louisiana possibly be next? Due to the lateness of the hour, and the slowness of the United States government to do anything, the governors concluded that it was better to ask for forgiveness rather than permission.

The bravado of war talk is always tempered by the reality of war talk. Now that everyone's cards were on the table, the players began to more seriously think about their next move. Jeb and Jeb Jr. hoped for the best but planned for the worst. They made a quick trip home to reassure their family that they knew what they were doing and would have each other's back. Jenny tried to maintain a stiff upper lip, but it quickly softened and quivered as she embraced her husband and son. "You two don't go taking any chances, now," Jenny pleaded. "I couldn't hit a nail on the head if my life depended on it," she advised Jeb. "And I have no clue how you trim hedges that straight," she confided to JJ.

"Don't worry dear, we'll be home before you know it," reassured Jeb.

"It'll probably not amount to anything, Mom. Mexico doesn't want to fight us," seconded JJ.

"Besides," Curtis chimed in, hoping to establish a more lighthearted tone, "I'll be here to tote that barge and lift that bale. You're in good hands with Curtis!"

"Are you sure you want to be a journalist? Maybe writing bad jokes is your thing," JJ suggested.

"Thank you for the vote of confidence. I will quote you in my next column, which would be my *first* column, actually," clarified Curtis.

"Don't go," cried Camilla, as she grabbed onto her dad and big brother. "Why do you have to go? Let someone else go."

"Would you let someone else do your book report, Squeaky?" JJ asked.

Camilla thought for a second, then said, "No, they wouldn't get it right!"

"Well, we want to make sure everything turns out right, too. A lot of men are counting on us to tell them what to do."

"Your father and brother are doing what they have to do, Camilla," asserted grandmother Taylor. "It's important to stand up for your friends and your country."

As everyone settled into the inevitability of the situation, Curtis' cell phone rang and he excused himself to answer it. "Hello, Curtis. Can you talk?" Amber asked.

"Not only that, I can sing and dance, too!" Curtis jauntily replied.

"You'll never change, will you?"

"Not unless you ask."

"Curtis, please. I've been watching the news. Will you be going into the Militia?"

"No, I'm not going anywhere. I still have my student deferment. How are things in Glocca Morra this fine day?"

"If that's a serious question, everything is as good as could be expected. Soon-Lee is fully recovered."

"And whatever happened with Omar?" Curtis followed up with true concern.

"His parents flew in from Pakistan. They took his body home with them. It was awful. Did they ever find out anything down there?"

"Not yet, but dad and I have an idea of what happened. We're looking into it."

"So how are you, Curtis? What are you doing?"

"I'll be doing Dad's job – and JJ's job- while they're gone. Or at least, try to do their jobs. In a perfect world, I'd like to get back to school."

"That's what I wanted to talk to you about, Curtis. As you know, I only have one semester left, so I sent out some resumes. Believe it or not, I got requests for interviews from two newspapers!"

"Who?"

"One is in New York, can you believe it? How fantastic is that!"

"That's great, Amber. How about the other one?"

"The other one is from right here in Chicago. I could be interested in that one, too, if…."

"If what, Amber?"

"If you were coming back to Kilmer. We could see each other and be together again."

"Well, that's hard to say right now, what with my job, or jobs here. Who knows when this will end. I'm really happy for you, Amber. Why don't we just wait and see?"

There was a moment of silence, then "Okay, Curtis. You're right. There's so much up in the air right now."

"Yes, there is," verified Curtis. "I'll call you."

"Okay. Good. I'll be here. Stay well, Curtis."

"You, too," Curtis replied and hung up, knowing he had come to the proverbial fork in the road. And all the signs seemed to be pointing in the same direction.

CHAPTER 31

THE TOWN OF SUGARFIELD, AND all communities across the Republic of Texas, hunkered down for war. Every able-bodied man who was not presently in the military parked his tractor, dropped his power tools or power-point presentation, and enlisted. Young women who were also qualified to join the Lone-Star State fighting forces did the same.

The esprit de corps that was welling up throughout the Republic was in direct proportion to the feeling of violation that had inspired it. The nation was up in arms, both figuratively and literally, over an action so calculated and cruel, all anyone could think of was "Payback!"

Everyone knew that the perpetrators had to have come from Mexico. The President of Mexico had to have been part of it. His country was known to be a cartel sympathizer and supporter. It was a training ground for drug running and terrorist activities. Everyone knew Pres. Jose Obrigon was guilty, until proven innocent, of supporting madmen of mass destruction, and he now had less than 24 hours to surrender these groups or suffer the consequences.

Curtis Moultrie was as outraged as anyone over the Port of Houston attack, but he questioned the knee-jerk reaction of invading an entire country in the name of retribution. Being a budding journalist, he tried to sift through all the impassioned rhetoric he was hearing in the hope of coming across some actual facts. What he knew was that a small group of individuals managed to somehow pull off a sneak attack of unimaginable magnitude. They obviously were martyrs who were ready to die for their cause. What cause? What had we done to them for them to take this inhumane action? Who were they?

The security camera footage from the docks that had been broadcast on TV showed one man slumped over the ferry boat wheel, one near the bow and a third man standing on top of the bridge with his arms raised in victory. The closer they got to their target, the clearer their images became. They were identifiable. Two of them didn't appear to be Hispanic. Maybe they were in a data base somewhere. Was anybody trying to find out? All anyone saw on TV was a justifiably outraged President McCall and an equally roiled and ready-for-action House of Representatives. All the speeches from the House members were wildly accusatory but lacking in facts. They parroted each other's incendiary remarks. No one in the chamber questioned the finger-pointing or table-thumping. It was almost as if no one dared speak in opposition to the manic views of the orators for fear of being labeled "Unpatriotic," and that wouldn't be good politics, especially for anyone who wanted to be re-elected.

Nevertheless, why the rush to judgment? Shouldn't there be an investigation? Who knows what facts might come out. Declaring war on a nation is risky business, notwithstanding the prevailing political attitude that "It will be over in a few weeks! People will be dancing in the streets!" Curtis didn't see the certainty in this line of thinking, but he felt like the Lone Ranger. Even the media didn't seem to share Curtis' reservations. No one was speaking out, calling for a more cautious response. Everyone seemed to be on the same page. The only question was one of comprehension.

Knowing he was in the middle of one of the biggest disaster stories of all time, Curtis began racking his brain for possible inside political sources that he could talk to. Then it hit him. His congressional district representative was a good friend – and liked to rub elbows with – Capt. Jeb Moultrie. Curtis thought he might be able to use his dad's name to wangle a short interview with Representative Hollingsworth. He thought right.

The representative from Ft. Bend County promised the fledgling journalist a 10-minute interview after the vote to go to war passed later in the day. Curtis arrived at the Congressman's office 2 minutes early, then waited 2 hours more. When Rep. Hollingsworth arrived, he apologized for the delay ("The battle plan briefing from the Secretary of War was anything but brief. It's a good one, though. We're ready!") He congratulated Curtis for having such a dedicated warrior for a father and asked how he might be of service.

Curtis briefly explained his view of recent events, to the obvious consternation of the Representative, and asked if there was anything to report about the identities of the bombers. "Not really," answered Hollingsworth. "We know where they came from. That's enough for us. Oh...and this is still classified information...but since you are a member of such a proud military family, I can tell you that we pulled the guy who set off the explosion out of the Channel. He was barely alive – and pretty delirious – but he kept mumbling a name: Jennifer. Jennifer Nelson. Probably his girl friend. Who knows. Who cares. We know where he came from. Got to go now. Say Hello to your dad and brother when you see them. They're great men. Follow their lead!" With a perfunctory hand shake and glance at his watch, Rep. Hollingsworth rushed off for his much anticipated date with infamy.

Curtis left the office and took a seat in the outer lobby as he tried to collect his thoughts. A light bulb was flickering in his head. The fact that one of the terrorists was alive was huge news. "But what about that name he mentioned," Curtis asked himself. "Jennifer...Nelson. Jennifer Nelson. I know that name. Where did I hear it?" Then came the dawn. "Rita!" he blurted out. Then to himself again, "JJ told us that Rita went to an abortion clinic recommended by a web site run by a Jennifer Nelson! Could it be the same person? What's the connection?"

Then, like any journalist worth his salt, Curtis grabbed his pad and pencil and headed for his next best source, a resource Woodward and Bernstein never had at their command: Facebook!

He powered up his computer and began by checking the abortion website that Jennifer Nelson ran. There she was, front and center, inviting pregnant Texas women who wanted an abortion, but couldn't get one in Texas, where it was reviled and totally illegal, to visit the Bessler Abortion Clinic in Norman, Oklahoma. There was a short paragraph about the rights of women to make their own decisions about their bodies and concluded with one final statement that read, "The rights of the individual are supreme. All oppressive nations must fall!"

"Really," Curtis thought, "that's a bit severe. There must be more to this story." The web site displayed quotes from many satisfied patients and offered a link to Jennifer Nelson's Facebook page for additional comments.

Curtis clicked on the connection and came face-to-face with dozens of quotable young women who were happy they went where they went. Men were listed, too. Most were simply being supportive of their girlfriend or wife. Some were as vociferous as Jennifer Nelson. One said, "The rights of the individual are supreme. All oppressive nations must fall." Curtis took a closer look at the small photo next to the quote. Take away the long, shaggy hair and beard and it was obviously a photo of a younger Mikhail Rasheed Wilson. Bingo!

Curtis Moultrie had uncovered a connection between two immensely impassioned individuals who believed in bringing down "Oppressive Nations." They used exactly the same phrase. Who are these people? Where did they come from? How had Texas oppressed Mikhail Rasheed Wilson? How could he follow up on this latest revelation?

Curtis decided to concentrate on the new Jennifer Nelson connection. Who else knew about her besides JJ and Rita? Of course! That investigative TV reporter knew about Jennifer Nelson. Rita had told her that's how she learned about the Oklahoma Clinic. Kay, that was her name. Kay Bailey at KXOTV. She has contacts. A lot of contacts. We could work together. Who knows what Moultrie and Bailey might turn up?

CHAPTER 32

ALL THE NETWORK NEWS BROADCASTS that evening were pre-empted by a message from President Melanie Ruthroff Simpson. Her tone was compassionate, heartfelt and unwavering.

"Good evening. On behalf of the people of the United States of America, I would like to express our feelings of great sorrow and sympathy to the people of the Republic of Texas over yesterday's terrorist attack on the Port of Houston. Our hearts and prayers go out to the families who lost loved ones in this cowardly and inhumane action.

It was not that many years ago that the city of New York suffered a similar, horrific blow. Today, we all feel your pain. It is from the depths of this shared experience that I ask the Republic of Texas to take pause and assess the circumstances of this tragedy. This is not the time to take any drastic action that you will regret later. Our nation made that mistake once before, and I do not want to see the Republic of Texas follow the same path. In fact, I insist.

None of us truly knows what happened here. And unless and until the country of Mexico is proven to be behind this terrorist attack, we will not allow any impetuous actions to be taken. In many ways, Mexico has become a good friend of the United States. It borders three of our states. We share business interests, travel opportunities and immigration agreements, and we will not tolerate any hostilities that may endanger lives or border relationships. The military buildup that is presently occurring must not be unleashed. I ask the Republic of Texas to stand down. Do not make this situation any worse than it already is.

We will be watching. God bless us all. And good night."

MQ-1B Predator drones from the Texas 146th Reconnaissance Wing crossed into Mexican airspace at dawn. These unmanned eyes in the skies began roaming the Mexican border, recording all vehicular traffic in search of suspicious convoys or other anomalies. Absent any particular evidence of encroachment, the mission was to identify targets of opportunity where subsequent missions could get the most bang for their buck.

On the ground, Capt. Jeb Moultrie was in command of Humvee units that were more decked out than a Rockefeller Center Christmas Tree. These expanded capacity war machines were fully optioned with Anti-Aircraft Missile Systems, M119 Howitzers, 3-barrel Gattling Guns and deep water fording kits. As a fighting force, Capt. Moultrie's hi-tech, heavily armored Humvee battle wagons could potentially take down a small country all by themselves, possibly even a sleepy, drug-addled country like Mexico.

The battle plan was to soften up the primary border crossings at Nuevo Laredo, Reynosa and Matamoros with "Stun and Gun" F-16 jet rocket attacks from the 150th Fighter Wing. The number of sorties flown would depend on the amount of damage inflicted and the response of the Mexican Army and Air Force. Other elements of the 150th Wing were assigned air border patrol duties and ordered to strafe any military vehicles heading to reinforce the border. The Humvees would follow, taking out targets of opportunity and mopping up.

Mexico had not fought a major war since the Mexican-American War of 1846 which lasted two years and resulted in the ceding of Mexican-held territory to the United States and the ultimate establishment of five new western states. Their nemesis, Texas, had previously won its independence from Mexico in 1836 and was now renewing the hostilities with a vengeance. The land of the Mayans and mariachis wasn't prepared for this.

Most of their army was centered in and around Mexico City. Their Blackhawk Helicopters and F-5 Jet Fighters would have their hands full against the advanced F-16 Fighter Jets from the Texas Air National Guard, the state-of-the-art Predator drones with their air-to-ground munitions and strike capability, and the weapons forces of the Texas State Guard, including 6 Regiments and 2 Air Wing Groups.

The Texas National Guard could pour thousands of infantry men into Mexico at the drop of a squadron of C-130 E Hercules Aircraft, with armored divisions and field artillery regiments to follow. A shootout at the Nuevo Laredo Corral didn't auger well for the Mexican gunslingers.

President Jose Obrigon maintained his country's innocence. He steadfastly denied any connection with the Port of Houston bombing and claimed that Mexico's pursuit of the drug cartels was making progress. He called on the United States to encourage peace in the region while his country's investigation of the terrorist attack took its course. Mexico had no citizenship records of Mikhail Rasheed Wilson, the one surviving terrorist. If he and his compatriots had entered Texas from Mexico, which was a distinct probability, their origin could have been Central America, and prior to that, who knows? Many of the drug cartels that run wild through Mexico come from South and Central America. Central America is also the dropping off point for insurrectionists from third world countries looking for easy access into the United States of America.

Invading Mexico would not address any of these issues, Obrigon argued. However, if any attack was launched, he promised his country would defend itself with an iron fist as lethal as the one that pummeled Spain into submission in 1821 to gain Mexico's independence. They would swallow up Texas like a red hot chili pepper.

Getting a better perspective on the big picture came from an unlikely alliance. Curtis Moultrie had come to trust Kay Bailey, as had a now obviously pregnant Rita Moultrie. The three of them held a conference call and put their heads together amid the bombast of approaching war. Curtis provided the name of the surviving bomber, Mikhail Rashhed Wilson, and the person he kept calling for, Jennifer Nelson. Rita provided the background on Jennifer Nelson as the person who recommended the abortion clinic and whom Rita was speaking with at the time of the clinic bombing. Kay had been looking into Jennifer's background based on the information Rita had provided two weeks earlier, and uncovered a history of foreign travel to Central America, a strange itinerary for an abortion rights advocate. Why did she go there? Who did she see? Could it have possibly been the man who couldn't get her off his mind, Mikhail? What are the odds?

The Moultrie-Bailey team believed they were onto something. It had to be more than mere coincidence that two of the people who were involved in the most violent atrocities to occur in and around Texas over the past few months somehow knew each other. The Oklahoma bombing was attributed to the Republic of Texas, and hostilities were on the verge of erupting between the United States and Texas. The Houston bombing was attributed to Mexico, and hostilities were on the verge of erupting between Mexico and the Republic of Texas – and again, between the United States and Texas. What was the one common denominator? The United States of America.

Someone was turning the screws on the relationship between the United States and the Republic of Texas. The purpose of this could be twofold: to force the U.S. to focus its attention and energies on Texas and precipitate violence between the two; and to foment another Civil War by possibly having other like-minded southern states join the fray.

The world knows that the United States would never fall to an outside invader. But what about delivering some devastating body punches? What about taking down your opponent from the inside? The most prescient president the United States ever elected was Abraham Lincoln, who made many providential statements, including: *"America will never be destroyed from the outside. If we falter and lose our freedoms, it will be because we destroyed ourselves."*

In the minds of Curtis, Kay and Rita, someone had turned the United States against Texas by orchestrating bombings in Oklahoma and in Houston. Could anyone be that shrewd? (Could anyone obscenely fly a country's airplanes into its own buildings after learning how to fly there?)

That "someone" had to be Mikhail Rasheed Wilson and Jennifer Nelson. How deep did this diabolical plot go? How could they find out more? After spending a sleepless night trying to flesh out their improbable but possible story, Kay Bailey showed up on the Moultrie doorstep the next day with the incriminating evidence they were looking for. After Curtis reassured his mother that Kay was now on their side, she went through everything she had discovered, step by step.

Late last night, Kay had returned to her TV station to look at the security camera footage from the Oklahoma bombing. All the cameras showed JJ and Rita racing out of the abortion clinic thirty seconds before the bomb went off. Then Kay looked through the log book of cell phones that had been turned in by individuals who had captured the aftermath of the blast. She reviewed the footage from each phone and found one that caught everything. It was the last phone turned in and seemed to have been ignored, possibly because of the preponderance of evidence. It required very close scrutiny, but the image was shot from the same side of the street as the clinic was on, and it showed JJ and Rita racing away from the clinic with their backs to the camera… followed by a third individual racing toward the cell phone camera just a few seconds before the blast of fire and smoke obscured everything.

After replaying the footage numerous times, there was no doubt about it. The third person who ran out of the clinic just seconds before the bomb went off was Jennifer Nelson. Jennifer Nelson had blown up the abortion clinic, not JJ Moultrie. Jennifer Nelson had set up JJ – and the Republic of Texas.

Kay Bailey paused, then told the rest of the story. "These are the travel itineraries," Kay explained as she methodically displayed the dossier of printouts, "that document the arrivals in Central America of both Jennifer and Mikhail," she continued, "on the same days four times earlier in the year," Kay concluded as she pointed out the most telling destination, "after spending six months together in Yemen – the international training grounds of Al-Qaeda."

CHAPTER 33

THE UNITED STATES OF AMERICA had seen enough. President Melanie Simpson's warning to the Republic of Texas had been ignored. Troops were massing at the Mexican border. Texas Air National Guard jets had over flown it. All it would take would be for one trigger-happy pilot – or commanding officer – to launch a phalanx of rockets and unleash the dogs of war which, as history has shown, will run wildly and uncontrollably, eluding capture for years on end.

President Simpson had been monitoring the worsening conditions at the border as she had promised, and concluded that she had no other choice but to heighten the nation's defense readiness condition from normal, or Defcon 5, to Defcon 3, which is only two stages above the all-out war footing of Defcon 1.

Furthermore, the United States established a no-fly zone which extended fifty miles south of a line running through the Rio Grande from the Gulf of Mexico to the western border at Juarez, Mexico. Any Texas Air National Guard aircraft that might venture into this air space would be immediately turned back by United States F-35 Lightning II Fighters or brought down, if necessary. President Simpson federalized the Arizona and New Mexico National Guards and ordered them to proceed to the border.

These actions did not sit well with President McCall of the Republic of Texas. He made his feelings known in a special news broadcast.

"24 hours ago, I gave President Jose Obrigon the opportunity to identify and surrender to us the terrorists responsible for the Port of Houston bombing. His silence has been deafening. We have proof that he is harboring madmen of mass destruction. We have the Smoking Gun. We have Mickhail Rasheed Wilson, the mastermind of the attack, in our custody. He, and two of his accomplices who died on their suicide mission, entered our country - from Mexico - with the express purpose of delivering a fatal blow to our infrastructure and instilling fear in the hearts of Texans, which as we all know who live here, is an impossible thing to do.

Nevertheless, this was a terrorist act from a country that aids and abets terrorism. This atrocity will be avenged, and we will not be stopped by anyone or anything – including the so-called No-Fly Zone. We will stand up against our enemies and administer the justice they so richly deserve. Time has run out for the perpetrators of terror and all who support them. Time has run out for Jose Obrigon and for Mexico."

Time was running out for Curtis & Company, too. The feisty team of inquiring minds had assembled some very weighty evidence showing that Mexico was not responsible for the Port of Houston bombing. According to their re-construction of events, the attack was an act of terrorism right out of the book of Al Queda.

Could they use more corroborating evidence? Yes. Did they need to know more about who else might be behind all of this? Absolutely. Did they have the time to follow through on anything? Absolutely not. As good as they were at putting this scenario together, they were by no means an intelligence network of trained spies. This was a job for the CIA or people at the Texas Department of War. Even if these agencies somehow agreed to become involved, it would still take time to figure out what had happened, and there was no more of that precious commodity left. Retribution was knocking on the door of indignation, and it was about to be answered.

Curtis didn't know where to turn. His dad and brother were at the front lines. His mother was too inextricably involved with her parents' health and the family finances to be burdened with the sensational facts that her son's new mini group had amassed.

Curtis' grandfather had slipped into the abyss of Alzheimer's. He needed almost constant attention, which his loving wife provided as best she could. Grandma Taylor's degenerating heart condition sapped much of her strength and all of their money. Like all of today's Texans, the Taylors had no national health care plan, no Social Security and no Medicare or Medicaid. Their medical bills were piling up and there was nothing they could do about it. Getting blood out of a turnip was still a biological impossibility. The only joyful moments the Taylors experienced these days were provided by Maria's recitations from the Bible and Camilla's rendition of the latest adventure fable.

Curtis took stock of the world he was now living in and did his best to lighten the load. "Mom, you need a break," Curtis advised as he sat down at the kitchen table with her and pushed the stack of bills aside.

"A break from what, Curtis? This is our reality now. Dad and JJ are gone, mom and dad are not well, and everything is going down the tubes," Jenny forlornly answered.

"Not if I can help it, mom. Let's figure this out. I can do more to help. I know money is a big problem, so let's do this: I can sell my car! It's in great shape. It's a real classic!"

"Curtis," his mother replied with an appreciative smile, "I could never ask you to do that."

"Why not? I don't need it. I'm not going back to school in the near future. Dad's and JJ's cars are here. How many cars do we need? We're not Hollywood stars! Mine's just taking up space. I'm putting an ad in the paper and online tomorrow."

"Curtis…" his mother tried to protest, "you don't have to do anything of the sort."

"Mom, I'm doing it. Period. End of statement. Exclamation point!!"

"I can help, too," Camilla chimed in. "I can sell my bike!"

"Camilla," her mom softly replied, "you're not selling anything!"

"I am so," insisted Camilla. "It's too small for me now anyway. I could get a lot of money for it. I'm a good ne-go-tia….negotiator!"

"Really," questioned Jenny, "and where did you learn that?"

"From Maria! She told me how her mom and dad would ne-go-tiate a better price for her clothes and things. They didn't have much money either."

"I would sell something, too, Mrs. Moultrie," Maria offered, "but I don't have anything."

"You girls are very considerate," Jenny replied as she began tearing up, "but we'll get by. There are a lot of people in the same boat."

"We have a boat?" a startled Camilla blurted out, "let's sell that!"

"No, honey, that's just a figure of speech. We don't have a boat."

"Good. I don't like boats. I'd rather have a new book!"

"That we can do, Camilla. You and Maria do so much around here, you both deserve a new book."

"Yeayy!" Camilla rejoiced, "I'll pick mine out tomorrow and read it to everybody!"

As everyone settled back in the warmth of their family togetherness, Curtis had another thought. "You know, mom, I can do more, too. Dad's and JJ's businesses are pretty much running on fumes. Our hourly workers can handle what's going on there and we'll still make a few dollars off of it. That way I can find a full-time job and help with all these never-ending bills. I know enough to work at a hardware store or lawn care company. I'm ready, I'm willing and I'm able!"

"I know you are, Curtis," his grateful mother replied, then changed her focus. "If only there was a way to keep us from going to war, and let everything get back to normal."

Curtis felt the wheels turning in his head as he replied, "Well, mom, since you brought it up, maybe there is a way. Maybe dad can help again. Let me fix you a glass of unsweetened iced tea and tell you what I have in mind."

Curtis spent the next ten minutes giving his mother the Reader's Digest version of his voyage to get to the bottom of the terrorist attack and his hope of getting two bickering adults together in the same room. Jenny was aghast and amazed, not only at the scope of the story she heard, but also at the fact that her free-spirited, witty son had been the driving force behind such a huge undertaking.

"Curtis, you amaze me," Jenny confided.

"That's what Jillian says….naw, just kidding, mom! All I'm doing is what I was born to do, I think. Everybody has a natural talent for something. You have to use it. I guess investigating things and writing about them is mine."

"Well, I hope your father can help. It just seems that things are so far along, I don't know if anybody's listening."

"I don't know either, mom. It's unbelievable the way people are so quick to judge others. There will always be some bad apples, but don't paint everybody with the same brush."

"Maybe you should major in psychology," Jenny replied, somewhat though not entirely, in jest.

"Nope! I'm looking forward to being an ink-stained wretch. Understanding people is part of that job, too."

"I only hope you can get through to the right people with your terrorist findings...*if* they'll listen."

"From your lips to God's ears," Curtis jauntily replied. "Gotta go now! I'm off to see the Wizard!"

Curtis bade his mother a warm farewell and set out to see what he could do to help resolve an international crisis, after which there would be plenty of time to resolve the crisis he had created for himself in his own life, otherwise known as his love life. Before hitting the road to Nuevo Laredo, he quickly phoned Jillian to tell her he was heading to the front lines at the border and not to worry. He would be thinking of her and he would be in touch soon. He quickly phoned Amber to tell her he was heading to the front lines at the border and not to worry. He would be thinking of her and he would be in touch soon.

Curtis Moultrie, the great diplomat, was about to embark on a mission of supreme importance to himself and to others. Right after he spoke with his dad.

CHAPTER 34

THE F-15 FIGHTER JET ROARED down the runway at Raklin Air Base
in San Angelo, Texas and took to the skies at daybreak. This mission was
anything but routine. Reconnaissance flights from the previous day had
revealed a possible build up of Mexican military vehicles and activity
around Ciudad Acuna, just across the border from Del Rio, Texas. In a
matter of minutes, the F-15 had arrived at its appointed co-ordinates and
circled at 15,000 feet.

Armed to the teeth with bombs, rockets and armor-piercing machine
gun ammo, it was one wild-ass, death-dealing freak show. By the time you
could say "lock and load," the bird of prey was dive bombing the target
for a closer look.

Men and machines on the ground scattered like a mound of fire ants
that had just been raked open. The F-15 pulled up sharply within 500 feet
of the ground, sending shock waves of ear-splitting decibels and searing
heat across the tarmac, then roared out of sight like a home run ball
powered by steroids. The pilot locked-in his target acquisition radar and
armed his on-board missiles. He flexed his shooting hand and completed
his 360-degree turn in preparation for final and fatal descent, when out of
the blue – and out of the sun – a United States Air Force A-10 Thunderbolt
II Attack Aircraft came bearing down on him like a laser beam from outer
space. And so did his wingmen.

The F-15 was hemmed-in and forced to level off and acknowledge the superior forces. The orders came through loud and clear: "F-15, you will disengage all weapons systems and set your course to Loxley Field, Alamogordo, New Mexico. We will escort you down. Over and out."

The landing at Alamogordo was uneventful, outside of the fact that the pilot was taken into custody, the plane was impounded and the Texas Secretary of War was apoplectic. His first chance to make a statement to the people and the president of Mexico was thwarted by United States sympathizers. "How dare they interfere with the affairs of a sovereign nation," Secretary Hextal bemoaned to his fellow cabinet members. "Was this an act of war? Is that what they want? The United States finally grants us our rightful independence, then they hang us out to dry when we're attacked, and then they defend the attackers! We will not be intimidated by anyone! We will not be deterred from accomplishing our mission. The Republic of Texas is not to be trifled with. They will see. Everyone will see the power and might of Texas justice!"

The Secretary was speaking for everyone in the room who felt sick and tired of being sandwiched between the rich and the poor; the powerful and the power less; the ungrateful and the unworthy. They would break out of this box and assert their independence once and for all. This fight wasn't over with. It was just beginning.

In an attempt to fight fire with fire, the Secretary of War ordered that new air missions be charted and flown through the No-Fly Zone and on into Mexico, only this time in squadrons of *three*. Simultaneously, all McCall's Militia units will proceed to the border, under air cover, and drive their Humvees into Mexico with rocket propelled grenades screaming and Gattling Guns blazing. Texas infantry units will seize control of all captured territories until Jose Obregon capitulates and the Mexican people can chart a new course, free from terror and oppression. The onslaught will be quick and decisive. The world will be a better place.

Or the world could be in a shambles if Mexico, Texas and the United States get into a three-way. What are the chances that cooler heads might prevail? What are the chances that the crux of this egoistic war-mongering could be exposed? Hello! Was anyone out there? Would anyone listen to the possibility that this was all one gigantic setup?

Three people who had every reason to think so were racing along in Jeb Moultrie's SUV, with Curtis at the wheel, in a last-ditch effort to talk to the powers-that-be in Laredo, starting with Curtis' dad. As they sped past military convoys and Humvee staging areas, Curtis implored everyone to get their act together. "I'll do the talking," he told Kay Bailey and Rita. "My dad will listen. If he asks, Kay, you show him what you found out and Rita, you tell him what you know. If he believes us, the hard part comes next: getting Col. Sloan to hear us out. He runs the militia. He can get to the higher-ups. I'm sure he'll be here, where the action is."

They got as far as downtown Laredo. All roads leading to the border from there were cut off by the military. Sentries were turning everyone back. When Curtis got up to the front of the line, he told the Corporal in charge who he was and asked him to contact Capt. Moultrie. After some hesitation, the Corporal finally agreed and got through to the Captain at his command post.

"He's not very happy that you're here," the Corporal advised as he handed the secure military phone to Curtis.

"Curtis, what the hell are you doing coming down here at a time like this! Why aren't you home looking after your mother?" his incredulous dad demanded to know.

"Dad, listen. Mom knows I'm here, okay? She thought I was crazy, too, at first. After I explained things to her, she agreed I should come see you. I've got information that could stop this insane war before it starts."

"Information? This is no time for information!"

"Yes it is, dad. That is exactly the point!" Curtis insisted. "We've uncovered the facts about what really happened in Houston. *Mexico didn't do it!*"

"What?" replied the incredulous Captain. "What do you mean, Mexico didn't do it. We got the guys on tape. We've got one in jail! They came from Mexico."

"Dad, they came *through* Mexico. They're not *from* Mexico."

"Who says so?" Capt. Moultrie defiantly asked.

"Kay Bailey, the investigative TV reporter, says so. Remember her? She's here!"

"You mean the woman who went after JJ for the bombing?" Jeb reminded himself. "He didn't do it!"

"She knows he didn't do it, dad. She knows who did! It's the same group that bombed the Port of Houston. Rita helped piece all this together. It's all on paper. Rita's here, too! She's pregnant for God's sake! That's how important this is, dad. We all know it. We've got to get this info to the top brass - The War Department! Can you get us 10 minutes with Colonel Sloan?"

"Hey, Curtis, that didn't go so well last time, remember?"

"That wasn't our fault, dad. People weren't listening then, either. They just wanted revenge. So, will you help us. All of us?"

Knowing he should immediately send his son back to Sugarfield, but also knowing he'd never hear the end of it if he did, Jeb managed a simple, "Alright, I'll try. The Colonel is here in the command post. Tell the Corporal up there to escort you down here. I'll see if I can get you five minutes. This is *not* proper military procedure, Curtis."

"No disrespect, dad, but that's my point exactly."

Fifteen minutes later, Curtis, Kay and Rita were presenting the evidence they had accumulated to Col. Sloan, commanding officer of McCall's Militia. Five minutes into the exercise, the Colonel held up his hand and said, "You people are truly amazing!"

"We try," Curtis replied, misinterpreting the military mind once again.

"First you question our immigration policies and now you're questioning our reasons for taking military action against a proven enemy! Three kids in an SUV know more about what's going on than we do?"

"We do have inside information, Colonel Sloan. Nobody knows about the connections between these people but us!" pleaded Curtis.

"Curtis, I know you mean well and I respect the hell out of your father, which is the only reason I'm talking to you, but I'm telling you that you are way over your head here. Go back to your home and your family, and take your crazy schemes with you. We're not interested in the facts. We've got our minds made up."

Finally coming to the realization that there was no way on God's big blue marble that he was going to convince anyone of anything, Curtis shrugged his shoulders, ceded the argument to the Colonel and his dad with a deferential nod, then gathered up his paperwork and his pals and got back on the road to reality. All the way back to Sugarfield, Curtis knew that any minute now, someone was going to fire the shot that started the war that killed all the people who had nothing to do with the hand that Al Qaeda dealt. And for the first time in his let's-get-to-the-bottom-of-this activist life, he felt totally helpless.

While Curtis and the Colonel were airing their differences, United States National Guardsmen from four different states had locked and loaded live ammunition and were heading for their battle with borderline chaos. At zero one-hundred hours, a convoy of 62 deuce-and-a-half trucks began arriving at the border in the event Texas followed through on its promised invasion. By sunrise, a battalion of battle-ready soldiers stood ready to enter the inflamed debate between antagonist and victim, although who-was-who remained an open question.

The likelihood of such an event materializing was enhanced by the up and down fist pump coming from the driver of the Humvee command vehicle, as Capt. Moultrie signaled his equally eager mobile charges to fall-in behind him. On any other day, the streets of Laredo are teeming with cars, trucks, prairie dogs and people. Today, it was deserted. A curious coyote poked its head out from behind a cactus, a prickly tumbleweed hopped, skipped and jumped hither and yon. The eerie silence was broken by the guttural groans of a dozen 400-horsepower engines filling the damp morning air with the acrid smell of diesel fuel.

This apocalyptic scene was being simultaneously repeated at four other border crossings, as Phase I of the invasion of Mexico was underway. As slowly as these heavily armored behemoths were advancing, just the opposite was happening high overhead as two dozen F-15 Fighters were approaching their rendezvous at nearly the speed of sound.

The drama mounted with every blink of an eye. The adrenaline flowed like hot lava. The tension was written all over the faces of the Mexican Army as they stepped out from their border posts into the middle of the street to confront the hated invaders.

Two hundred miles away, on a front porch filled with family members, Curtis looked to the south with the apprehension of a deep sleeper caught in the quicksand of a nightmare.

The shot heard around the world rang out from the most unexpected quarters. Capt. Moultrie heard it as he came to a halt close enough to the face of Commander Benito Juarez to count the hairs on his moustache. Curtis Moultrie heard it as he slowly rose from the wicker chair on the front porch, and everyone at the border heard it as they all realized the day of reckoning had arrived.

CHAPTER 35

IT STARTED WITH A STREAK of crackling, blinding light, stinging winds and the roar of an approaching freight train, followed by a whistling, shrieking banshee that came screaming out of the sky like a demon from another world. It reached down from the heavens like a sinewy, undulating wormhole digesting everything, leaving nothing, as it snaked through the defenseless plains, otherwise known as "Tornado Alley."

It was a tornado of epic proportions, registering an EF-5 on the Enhanced Fujita Scale, with winds in excess of 200 miles per hour. It was over a mile wide, savagely heading east. And there were several of them.

Jeb Moultrie looked skyward, transfixed by the roiling, angry dark green clouds that were giving birth to a seething, screeching monster. Capt. Moultrie and Commander Juarez gave each other a quick glance and realized in that moment that they were standing in each other's shoes, in the same place and time on the same hideous path to hell. They gave each other an anxious farewell nod and turned to their men.

"Fall back!" Capt. Moultrie shouted out amid the rising roar. "Take cover!" he commanded, which was easier ordered than done. Everyone was out in the open, exposed to the sucking tentacles that were grabbing at the very fiber of every man's being. Startled Humvees backed off the road, and into each other, in their frantic attempts to escape impending doom. Some foot soldiers took refuge under the bridge leading to the Rio Grande, others sought safety beneath the undercarriage of helpless Humvees, now reduced to playing a defensive role, like a bald eagle protecting her nest.

The earth shook as the mother of all suckers proceeded to pick and choose its intended victims. Humvees were levitated and tossed into a pile. Buildings were vaporized. Cattle were being shown how to fly. Men from both armies were discharged like cannon fodder as the beast cleared a pathway through humanity the way a hungry school boy cleans his plate.

Capt. Moultrie sat helplessly behind the wheel of his Humvee as it flipped and flew in fits and starts like a simulated rocket ship ride at a space museum. He came to rest upside down in the Rio Grande. Of all the capabilities built into the M1113, inverted floating was not one of them, and Jeb's favorite ride began sinking like a rock. His broken collarbone was excruciatingly painful as he banged his body against the jammed door. Jeb looked over and saw that the passenger door had been blown off, taking Zeke with it. The Rio was pouring in but Jeb managed to fight through the rising tide and force his injured body to the surface. Now floating in the waters that separated the Hatfields from the McCoys, he surveyed the scene ashore. It looked like the surface of the moon: barren ground, scattered rocks and boulders, no sign of life. No flags, no tire tracks, no footprints in the sand. On either side of the river.

He arduously dog paddled his way to the shore and crawled up the river bank. Jeb got to his feet and looked in all directions. To the east, he could see the EF-5 bobbing and weaving its way toward the next community, rendering unto itself all of man's works and deeds. Its path of destruction was complete. The meandering monster had left miles of death and heartbreak in its wake. The defeated Captain sat down in the middle of the devastation and prayed for the souls of the men and women who had lost their hopeless battle against the forces of nature and for those who were awaiting a similar fate soon to be meted out by two more funnel clouds forming farther north. And those were just the ones he could see.

In the safety of small-town Sugarfield, the Moultrie family had been listening to the emergency weather reports. They knew what had happened at the border. They were justifiably worried about the fates of Jeb and JJ and the others. All cell phone service was out. There were no reporters anywhere near the scene. Traffic copters and small planes near Laredo from airfields that survived were preparing immediate flyovers. Laredo and Nuevo Laredo in Mexico were the hardest hit. An EF-4 with winds exceeding 166 mph touched down in Falfurrias and Kingsville. And to the north, another one was bearing down on Houston. The city that runs on oil took another gut shot as the tornado first roared through the city proper, tearing apart the Alamodome as though it was made out of papier mache then careening through the business section like a drunken sailor before exiting stage right over the remains of the Port of Houston. It's wild twin sister showed up a few miles to the south, acting out on the road to Sugarfield.

Curtis went outside to scan the skies and was driven back inside by a real-life wind tunnel and sideways torrent of rain and hail. He gathered up his mother, grandparents, little sister and her friend and headed for the smartest addition his father ever made to their home: the storm cellar. They squeezed into the underground cocoon and huddled together as the tornado roared out their names. Their cries went unheard as the maniacal whirling dervish passed overhead and sucked the life out of their neighborhood on its way to its final resting place in Galveston Bay.

As the raging beast took its last breath and died, the Moultries cautiously re-entered the world around them and didn't recognize any of it. Entire city blocks had been razed. Furniture had been re-arranged in trees. Knives and forks were embedded in trunks. Some homes were left untouched. Others were sliced in half. Theirs was missing part of its roof, most of the garage and a kitchen wall had been ripped clean off. Water was gushing from broken pipes. They walked around weeping in the silence, examining their relatively untouched possessions and thanking God for saving them from what might have been. Curtis shut off the main water supply and began taking stock of their immediate needs. A roof over their head was mandatory. Where would he start? What would his dad do?

The only good news to come out of a day of atrociously bad news was that no tornadoes had formed west of Laredo. The thousands of National Guard troops at the New Mexico/Mexico border were unscathed. The EF-5 had done what no human interaction was able do: it stopped the war in its tracks. Hundreds of lives lost would be a lot easier to assimilate, and justify, than thousands.

Capt. Moutrie's unit was decimated. His Humvee was lying on its back in the Rio Grande like an overturned tortoise on the beach. Three others had met a similar fate, but JJ's was still up and running. He had had the temerity and good luck to out-maneuver the EF-5 on the back roads of Laredo like a race car in a demolition derby. His version of taking the checkered flag was sighting his dad sitting all by his lonesome in the middle of nowhere. He gunned his bruised and battered Humvee into the wake of the killer tornado and spun a flamboyant donut in front of his dad's wondering eyes.

Jeb looked at his son with the same miraculous sense of awe that he felt at the moment of his birth. They didn't say a word or waste a minute as they grabbed each other in a bear hug that was as intense as the pain from Jeb's broken collar bone.

"Dad, you're hurt!" JJ suddenly realized.

"No big bag of wind is going to bring me down. That mindless monster is dead and gone and I'm still standing," Jeb proudly proclaimed.

"How about the rest of the unit?"

"Most of the guys made it," JJ answered. "A couple of bumps, bruises and broken bones. Two are MIA."

"Plus Zeke," Jeb added. "He got blown out like a candle."

"Wow. Poor guy. He was a fighter," JJ reflected. "He always had your back. Same with the Humvees. Most of them are kind of mangled, but they did give us some protection."

"Can't say the same for the Mexicans," Jeb added, looking across the big river with a strange sense of kinship. "It looks pretty desolate over there."

"What other towns got hit?" JJ wondered. "How far did these things go? I hope not all the way up to Sugarfield!"

"We've got to find out," Jeb said, clutching his aching shoulder. "Let's get to a phone. Better yet, fill this baby up," Jeb instructed as he painfully climbed aboard JJ's war wagon-turned ambulance. "And floor it!"

As is the case with tornadoes, if you are in their path, you will suffer the consequences. If you are not, you won't. Only twenty minutes after leaving a scene that looked like a bombed out city from WWII, they came across untouched civilization, with working gas stations and cell phone towers. Jeb checked in with his boss, Colonel Sloan, who had remained safe in the command center, and told him all his men were accounted for and that he was heading home as fast as his chopped, dropped, and banged up set of wheels could get him there.

Sloan gave him the green light and two hours later Jeb and JJ roared into Sugarfield in a cloud of dust and debris. The town looked like a crazy quilt, with one house here, a missing one there, another house across the street, and a second lot bare.

They pulled up in front of their own home and marveled at the fact that it was still standing. They rushed inside to find everyone sitting around the dining room table as though dinner time was only a dinner bell away, going over a list of things to do. They all leapt out of their chairs and burst into tears at the sight of their returning heroes. There were reassurances of good health all around, and they all thanked their lucky stars for that. Jeb wasted no time in placing a call to his long-time building materials supplier, which was still open for business, and ordered the lumber and shingles for the roof and the exterior-grade plywood for the walls for immediate delivery.

In the meantime, Curtis and JJ gave their dad a hand in bringing down the rolls of plastic sheathing that he had stored in the attic to cover the hole in the roof and tack up a temporary kitchen wall. Camilla and Maria vacuumed all the carpeting and swept up the kitchen floor. Grandma and grandpa Taylor recalled the tornadoes of '86 and Jenny put on a pot of coffee before filling the pots and pans with whatever she had on hand to feed a party of nine.

If ever there was a day to be thankful, this was it. Jeb thanked the Lord for the bounty before them and for saving them from the terror behind them. The country ham, sweet potatoes and collard greens never tasted so fine. Curtis recounted his futile efforts to save the planet from war, only to have the outcome he desired fulfilled in the harshest of ways by a cantankerous mother nature. John and JJ re-lived their worst nightmare and remembered the men who succumbed to it.

"I think Zeke knew his number was up," Jeb said aloud. "Just before the wind sucked him out the door he admitted to me he was the one who shot that kid from Pakistan on the steps of the Capitol. Kind of like we thought, JJ. His mind was all messed up from the Iraq war. He had that Post Traumatic Stress problem. Anytime he saw a Middle Eastern-looking person, he flashed back to the firefights he had over there. In his mind, that kid, Omar, was the enemy. And he shot him. He was sorry as hell. I told him I understood. And then he was gone."

The silence in the room signified everyone understood. Jeb would explain everything to the police.

As the sun went down on a day no one would ever forget, the thoughts of all the adults in the room turned to the question of how they would pay the piper for the dance he led them through. Not just in their case, but for those who had nothing left at all. There was no insurance for this. Other than charity, and neighbor helping neighbor, how could anyone pay for what had happened here? Medical services would be taxed. Medical bills would be astronomical. Clean up bills, too, would be in the millions. Where would some of these people live? There was no FEMA anymore. Texas couldn't count on any help from the outside world. It was sink or swim time. Which reminded Jeb, he better have someone take a look at that collar bone.

CHAPTER 36

SOME PEOPLE IN THE UNITED States couldn't have cared less when Texas left the union. Some understood their thinking but not their conclusion. Others likened their departure to a disgruntled youth who had run away from home out of spite. In any case, everyone felt deep sympathy for the people who had suffered the effects of the great Texas tornadoes. Some had donated money and clothes to the local charities. Some volunteered their services. The President of the United States summed up the prevailing attitude in America as Melanie Ruthroff Simpson appeared on national TV.

"Good evening my fellow Americans and good evening as well to the citizens of the Republic of Texas. Once again, I come to you on a solemn occasion and a matter of great importance. On behalf of the citizens of the United States, I would like to offer our deepest sympathies to the people of Texas who had the misfortune to suffer through yet another horrendous incident. This time it was unforeseeable and unpreventable. The tornadoes that decimated so many Texas communities could have happened anywhere. It is a human tragedy.

And as such we would like to offer you a helping hand. As you know, we sent thousands of National Guard troops to your borders to prevent a war which, thankfully, never materialized. I am now offering to make these troops available to you to help with your rescue and clean up efforts throughout Texas.

Furthermore, as a humanitarian gesture, I am offering to send representatives from FEMA into Texas to ascertain and provide any immediate needs for temporary housing for your dislocated citizens.

Finally, and most important, I would like to point out that there are forces in today's world which have been acting against our best interests, and yours, in an effort to pit us against each other and weaken our defenses. As you now know, the recent bombings of the Oklahoma Abortion Clinic and the Port of Houston were the acts of a terrorist cell that originated in Yemen. We learned these facts through a news reporter's investigation, the subsequent involvement of our own intelligence community plus a concerned citizen of yours.

Imagine how much easier we could have defused this situation had we all been working in concert from the beginning. Additionally, we know your economy is hurting and your social services are, too. Therefore, I believe it is in both of our best interests that you rejoin our union of states. Our working at cross purposes plays right into the hands of devious-minded terrorists. Returning your absent star to our field of blue would require a two-thirds vote of Congress, which should easily pass plus a majority vote of your citizens in order to make this marriage official. The door is open to a fresh start and a united front against terrorism.

As Thomas Jefferson once said, *"The purpose of government is to place before mankind the common sense of the subject, in terms so plain and firm as to command their assent and to justify ourselves in the independent stand we are compelled to take."*

Good luck, good night and God bless."

The meeting of the U.S. and Texas armies at the New Mexico and Texas border wasn't anywhere near as confrontational as the stare down was between Capt. Moultrie and Commander Juarez back at the Mexican border. The orders came down and the fences came down as National Guardsmen from New Mexico and Arizona happily joined forces with McCall's Militia on the road to Laredo and points east. The state of Texas hadn't seen a convoy this celebrated since the Dallas Cowboys won the Super Bowl, and the results were just as satisfying as soldiers in uniforms of different colors and stripes worked together clearing the land and building shelters for the grateful living.

FEMA showed up at every impoverished city, setting up the trailers and services that were so desperately needed. All across the Republic of Texas, people were opening their minds to the idea that *One Nation, Under God*, might be worth another try. President McCall wasn't entirely convinced.

"My fellow Texans, it was with a heavy heart that I witnessed the catastrophe that occurred in Tornado Alley. We pray for a speedy recovery of the injured and rapid rebuilding of our people's homes and lives.

We thank President Melanie Simpson for providing the troops, equipment and supplies to facilitate our recovery.

As to her observations regarding the threat of Al Qaeda that we both face, all I can say is we are ever watchful in the defense of our nation. Though our methods may have been different, we had every intention of getting to the bottom of the recent attacks on our people and property. Re-joining the union may be a bigger step than we need to take at this time.

Nevertheless, as in all great democracies, it will be put to a vote. We voted for sovereignty in 1836 and again in 2007. Whatever the outcome of this new ballot, I shall abide by the will of the people, so help me God. Thank you and good night."

Arguments were made for and against the United States' annexation of Texas by Texas media commentators (evenly split), economic analysts (pro), and politicians (con). As predicted by President Simpson, Congress achieved the two-thirds vote necessary for passage. Then the people of Texas were heard from. The results proved to be far less than a landslide but more than a simple majority, as reflected in the reactions at the Ft. Bend County Fairgrounds the day after the vote was announced.

The celebration was up-beat and widespread. The marching bands were back, along with the firecrackers and patriotic festivities. Everybody was there. Curtis and Jillian shared their blue cotton candy with each other. A very pregnant Rita watched JJ bob for apples. Jeb and Jenny sat on a bench next to grandma and grandpa Taylor and Camilla carried around a fuzzy top hat with a cat inside. The news media were out in full force interviewing the locals on national TV.

Curtis and Jillian happily answered the reporter's questions on camera and arm-in-arm. Hundreds of miles away, an attractive young African American woman was watching the proceedings on TV, holding an open package and note she had just received in the mail. Tears were flowing down her beautiful face as she recognized Curtis and Jillian and saw how happy they were together.

She looked down and read the note one more time. It said, "Amber – Follow your dreams! Love, Curtis." The present that came in the box was a pretty, silk designer scarf with many colorful hearts surrounding the phrase: "*I love New York!*" Amber tied on the scarf, turned back to the TV and managed a wistful smile.

Some special guests had come in for the occasion. They included Kay Bailey, now a very well-known TV reporter from Oklahoma, FBI Special Agent Roger Wilkins and his wife Suzie from Atlanta, Frank and Emma Kazmarczyk from Iowa and Hector and Juanita Estrada from Reynosa, Mexico. They all had stories to tell and they were more than happy to tell them, as the crowd listened with great interest.

All around the fairgrounds, people were taking in this historic day. Some were very happy, some were not so happy, some were waving their Gadsden flags, some were wearing their Lone Star shirts, but all the individual celebrations ceased when the marching band struck up The National Anthem, and the flag that everyone had come to see was hoisted on high in the center of Ft. Bend County, Texas.

It was the stars and stripes of the United States of America.

CHAPTER 37

IN THE WEEKS AND MONTHS that followed, Jeb Moultrie Construction came roaring back, big time. There was a need for new construction all around Sugarfield, and Jeb had more work than he could handle. JJ chipped in when he could, although his landscaping business was going great, too.

The Moultrie home looked better than ever with a new roof, enlarged garage and expanded kitchen. Jenny loved the new appliances and pushed them to their limits every weekend. Grandma and grandpa Taylor were able to move in to an assisted living facility less than a mile from the house. Camilla had fallen in love with <u>Alice in Wonderland</u> and was given a cat for her birthday which she immediately named *"Cheshire"*. Maria was living with her parents again just a short drive away. And Curtis made amends with Jillian, went back to school and wrote a book.

He collaborated with Kay Bailey in his free time. It was entitled: <u>Deceit and Conceit </u>by Moultrie and Bailey, and it was the complete story of the Oklahoma Abortion Clinic and Port of Houston bombings. Now the hard part, finding a publisher, was coming along, too. Curtis had received a call from Burris Publishing in New York. Apparently, one of their up-and-coming journalists from an affiliated newspaper, named Amber Jones, had recommended his book. He had an appointment with the publisher in a week, after which he planned on doing some sightseeing.

In addition to the usual trips to the Statue of Liberty and Empire State Building, Curtis had heard about an exciting new attraction.

All he needed was for someone to give him good directions to the fantastic new Ferris Wheel at Coney Island.

##